ISBN 0-943864-47-X

DATE DUE

SENIORITIS

by

TATE THOMPSON

MAY DAVENPORT PUBLISHERS

Los Altos Hills, California U.S.A.

May Davenport Publishers
26313 Purissima Road
Los Altos Hills, CA 94022

Library of Congress Control Number: 2003106136

ISBN 094386447X

First Edition

Printed in the U.S.A.

Cover by Kara Bang

Dedication

I would like to dedicate "Senioritis"
to my wife, Meriam
and
my son, Hogan.

For my wife, Meriam, thank you for supporting
my dreams when others didn't.

For Hogan, you are our everything.

"SENIORITIS"

Nakeisha

Don't think you know me, cuz you don't.

Mr. T says I have to write to get what I be thinking down on paper so I ain't offendin' no one and he say that's what the principals want for me.

Mr. T says that sometimes you just have to "play the game." I'll play the game for Mr. T cuz he the blackest white dude I ever seen and he really knows us. There ain't no other teachers that unnerstan' us like he do, so don't go thinkin' I be doin' this shit for no Mr. Punk-Ass Principal.

Anyway, Mr. T says I need to get my thoughts down on paper and I agree cuz I have a hard time keepin' my mouth shut when mother f-...Okay, let me say that a different way. Mr. T says I got to censor myself. I have a hard time keepin' my mouth shut when adults that think they in charge around here start tryin' to tell me what I gotta do.

They don't know me, cuz if they did, they would recognize that Nakeisha runs da' show and ain't no one can say some educated sh-...

Okay Mr. T., damn. Even when I ain't talkin' out loud I can hear Mr. T's voice in my head tellin' me I gotta approach adult leaders differently.

Ain't no one can say no blasé blasé stuff that I know they can't make work. High schools don't got no rules for niggas like me cuz I know they

1

can't follow through with half the shit they say they gonna do. I just say, look, you discriminatin'...and they back off and I stay in control.

The problem is that I been assigned this 3-5 program cuz I'm sposed to be a senior and I'm missing some credits. Mr. T says that if I don't lower my pride and kiss Ol' Dude's ass for awhile, I ain't gonna graduate and they all gonna be happy cuz they think "kids like me" are better suited for working at Click-n-Ship and stayin' out of they hair.

A'ight Mr. T, I'm getting' to the point. Man, sometimes he makes me feel like I'm some schizo cuz I hear his voice in my head like he be my conscience or some shit. Part of what I be doin' in this 3 to 5 program is earning my credits. The other part of what they say I'm sposed to be doin' is changin' my attitude.

First of all, I ain't got no attitude, but Mr. T say that I got to "play the game," so I'll go along with it for him.

One of da things that Ol' Dude wants me to do is write a letter to this school that says how I think I deserve to graduate and why, and why me? I ain't wrote no letter yet, but I guess I'll do it for Mr. T. They is lucky that he be here, though. If he wasn't here I wouldn't even think about no damn letter. I'd tell them to go f-...I'd tell them to get out my face and if they kept talkin', I'd get loud and that's what Mr. T says they want me to

2

do, so they got some excuse to get rid of me.

Anyway, I got to write this damn letter and I ain't got no idea what I'm gonna say yet cuz they don't know me and they ain't got no business knowin' what I be thinkin'. It ain't none of their damn business.

"What now Mr. T?"

"Did you just write..."

"Yeah, I just wrote it ain't none of their damn business."

"Nakeisha, you know I think you are a great kid."

"Yeah, we cool."

"I understand that part of your persona is that attitude you try to play for your friends."

"Mr. T, why you always tryin' to analyze shit?"

"I see it as part of my job. Look, you are a beautiful girl whom a lot of the teachers prejudge because you get loud when you want to be heard. I am used to that. They aren't."

"True."

"You also know that you intimidate teachers and your peers when you get loud. When you get loud, you look like you could get aggressive and that scares people. So, with your friends you get your way because they are scared and with your teachers you get thrown out of class, right?"

"True, true."

"Okay, back to your writing that it is none of

their damn business. Don't you find it a little strange that you say something is 'none of their business' and then whenever they confront you, you get all in their business and start insulting them, and then you go ahead and tell them all of your business too."

"I know Mr. T, but they be hasslin' me and tryin' to discipline me one second an' get all up in my head the nex."

"All I am saying is that you need to tone down the attitude for a few months, graduate, and then you can tell them where to go. But, only do that after you have the diploma in hand."

"I know what you sayin' Mr. T, but these adults try to boss me aroun' an-..."

"Nakeisha! It's stuff like that that keeps you in trouble."

"I know Mr. T, but I get tired of people always tryin' to tell me that they know me and they gone do what's best for me. How they know what's best for Keisha?"

"Look, I know I can't convince you to like other adults in the building, but you like me right?"

"Yeah Mr. T, I tole you we cool. You ain't like no other white dude I ever seen."

"Okay Keisha, I'll admit that a lot of teachers enjoy getting certain kids suspended or kicked out of school and you are one of their main targets. You are black, you are loud, you challenge anything you think is unfair, and I love you for all

4

of those things; but, those are the things that certain adults in our high school use to squash kids like you."

"Mr. T, you just lay it all out there. I know you got to be one of us."

"Look Keisha, you have a gift for expressing yourself. You know when you all do that blaze battle stuff in the parking lot?"

"Yeah, we be mad clownin' all the boppers in the school and all them cakes that be thinkin' they's playas."

"You realize that the reason you win isn't just because you are funny. You have a talent with words."

"You think so Mr. T?"

"Yeah, I think so. You have more natural intelligence than most kids in this school."

"Thanks Mr. T, that's why you my dawg and we always gonna be cool."

A'ight, Mr. T done talkin' to me, I'll get to the point. I'm a senior and I'm gonna walk across that stage cuz my whole family's already comin', and I can write some shit that'll make Ol' Dude happy, but I ain't doin' it today because some nerdy little black dude with a wild fro and taped glasses say he need to borrow some paper from dis' notebook.

Gemini

Here I sit, pondering the ramifications of my recent juvenile impulsiveness. Mr. Tompkins has communicated his opinion on the "powers that be" and the reasons for their recent requests. My placement in the 3-to-5 program stems from dubious disciplinary policies.

In order for me to have acquired a position in the "much put-upon," or 3-to-5 program, I scuffled with a few fellow young men over their intrusion of my position in the lunch line. I thought that I had properly internalized my anger, which was based on the lack of time I had to eat because of the invasion and overtaking of my spot in line.

I did not realize that I had hit my breaking point. I decided that the aforementioned incidents were in dire need of closure. Therefore, I decided against evasive action and actively pursued the quick obliteration of further human conflict.

As soon as my place in line was infiltrated, I quickly subdued the assailants with a barrage of fists, which quickly changed my peers' demeanor and drew the school security closer to me than I preferred. I remained in my pugilistic pose as I was extricated from my position in line, which ironically was my goal for my peer perpetrators and not for me.

The inherent problem I see with my placement

in the 3-to-5 program is that I have no prior offenses. I am an excellent student who was caught in the crosshairs of those who have no respect for their peers' personal space. I view my landing in the 3-to-5 program as a clear act of prejudice. The principal the other kids call "Lurch" seems to have something against young black males. The percentage of kids suspended for AWB (Attending While Black) by Lurch is overwhelmingly higher than the groups of kids guilty of the same offenses from any other race.

Nonetheless, I will write the letter the administration requires, complete my senior class project, and do my assigned time in the 3-to-5 program.

In addition, Mr. Tompkins says I may tutor some of my peers in the 3-to-5 program and I feel as though that will make my time more worthwhile for my fellow offenders and me. I am still deciding what to write in my letter, but it will take awhile and Mr. Tompkins asks that I write on a level that the administration can understand. He says he is going to give me an example of how to accomplish the aforesaid forthwith.

Ricky Terrell

Mr. T just told me that I have to write a letter to the administration, do extra community service and recover four credits by the end of the semester in order to graduate. Not like any of this matters because I have a full-ride football scholarship to Kansas State and I'm gonna go pro in a couple of years.

I don't know why all these people at this school think they can tell me how to live. Have any of them ever played D-1 ball? I don't think so. If one more cake dude tells me that I am screwing up my life, I think I am going to be sick.

I think that just because I am half black, some people think that I am the stereotypical coddled player with no brains. I am smarter than any of these people know. I don't use Ebonics, and I don't have to act black to be black.

At least this 3-to-5 program looks like it is going to be entertaining to me. This Gemini dude is around my intelligence level and Nakeisha is like a walking Blaze Battle. Patrick is pretty humorous, but you can tell he never had to want for anything. Jamal thinks he's funny, but I haven't laughed at anything but his size so far. LaStacia is obviously here for me to score.

At least this semester will be fun. These people have to pass me because I am the person they will have to live their pathetic lives through. God knows none of the staff here could ever accomplish what I am going to.

All right, this ought to suffice for Mr. T. I am going to stop writing now because this crazy white dude is trying to pick a fight with Nakeisha.

Hell, I'm huge and I don't even want to test her. She's just plain scary. I need to tell Coach Snyder to leave a scholarship open. Keisha could be a helluva linebacker.

"Shut up you oompa loompa looking scary little leprechaun man!" Nakeisha announces with a smirk on her face, finger held above her head pointing in a downward fashion.

"Why don't you shut up you oversized Amazon lady!" replies Alex in a voice fading in and out of manhood.

"All right guys, knock it off!" says Mr. T., and Nakeisha and Alex quickly calm down. Mr. T gives Nakeisha the look and says, "Nakeisha, come here."

"What Mr. T?"

"Why do you insist on messing with everyone? You know that Alex has issues and baggage, why do you test him?"

"Just cuz he got issues, don't mean he got no right to get in my face."

"Okay Keisha, you're right, but I told you that you need to start to choose your battles more wisely. You get into a fight with Alex right here right now and you will find yourself out of school wishing that you had your diploma."

"Mr. T, just because someone say Alex got problems, don't mean that give him the right to get in my face, do it?"

"No Keisha, but it also doesn't give you the

right to instigate by calling him a little oompa loompa leprechaun man."

"True, true."

"Okay then, do we have an agreement that you will stop clowning on people as long as you are in the 3-to-5 program?"

"I'll agree to that if you draw up a contract that everyone have to sign."

"Okay Nakeisha, I'll make up a contract, but if you sign this and then make a habit of violating the contract, I will write you up and you'll be out of here, which is the last thing I want. But, don't think that you are getting any special privileges from me. I know how you usually work the principals by saying they are discriminating against you. But, you can play the race card all you want with me and I won't back down. Because of you, I have about 100 kids that will be right there to take up for me too. Believe that!"

"Alright Mr. T, just make up the contract and I'll be good while I'm in 3 to 5, but I won't promise anything for day school."

"Fair enough. The contract is going to say that if you clown on anyone in here, or if they clown on you, that the person doing the clowning will be in violation of the contract, and will have to do whatever I ask of them in order to get reinstated and not written up."

"A'ight den. You got a deal, Mr. T, but don't think you special just cuz you won this time. I still think you cool, but that leprech-..."

"Nakeisha!"

"Okay, Mr. T, I'm straight now. Believe that! Ha ha! On the real though Mr. T, if you was any other teacher in this school, you know I'd be clowning again as soon as I got through signing. But, since it's you and you is a brother inside, I'll be straight for now."

Patrick Matthews

I can't believe I ended up in the 3-to-5 program. These are the kids that I used to make fun of for being slackers and thugs. Man, this sucks. If Miss Becker hadn't decided to make me an example for plagiarism, I would have never ended up in this place. My girlfriend is embarrassed and my mom will never forgive me for this.

My mom is still pretty upset about me losing my position as National Honor Society president. They voted me out last week because my plagiarism incident was a clear violation of the honor code. I just can't believe that Miss Becker decided that what I did was worth taking to the administration. Hell, I have always written my research papers like this. Half the class was guilty, but I guess I was just too damn honest, so I got in trouble.

I now have no chance of being salutatorian. I knew that Gemini would be the valedictorian, but

I had my life planned.

I had Gemini in my English class as a freshman and as a junior. To the outsider, Gemini might be considered a nerd, especially when he was a freshman. Gemini has his hair in little twists that make him look Jamaican. He is a wiry person with pants that are generally an inch or two too short. He wears glasses that are always broken and taped in some way. He forgets to bring his materials to class. He wears his sister's oversized coat, which doesn't match anything he owns. Oh yeah, Gemini is a genius and he could possibly fit every stereotype known to man; however, Gemini seldom gets made fun of because everyone is in awe of him.

It always takes those who haven't met him a few minutes to get used to his slow, deliberate talking. Most students are dumbfounded after listening to him speak for awhile. Gemini has the vocabulary of a college student and the insight of someone three times his age.

Gemini has always been my favorite person to hear read out loud in my classes. He could easily be one of those people who do books on tape. Gemini is able to change his voice to fit the characters speaking, and he uses the perfect cadence every time he reads. Then, as soon as he is asked a question about what he has read, he explains in such exquisite detail that the kids think he is a god.

One of the other factors that keeps Gemini

from being made fun of like the typical nerd is that he can dance like Michael Jackson in his prime. Our school loves to watch talented people perform and Gemini is multi-talented. He is also an unbelievable dramatic and comedic actor in the school plays. He actually wrote and acted in a one-act play for the annual school talent show.

Gemini is a unique, which means that he melts down all stereotypes and generalized norms by being the exception to every rule. In other words, I didn't mind having to settle for salutatorian, but now even that is blown.

So what was the use of me getting all "A's" all the way through school, if I was going to blow it right at the end? At least it won't hurt my chances of getting college scholarships because I already applied for those before any of this happened.

I guess you could say I have a slight case of senioritis because aside from the fact that my mom is devastated, I don't care about anything but getting this shit over with as soon as possible. All I care about for the rest of the year is going to the prom with my girlfriend Jacque Jones, and project graduation. Everything else is just a waste of my time. I still get credit for history while I am in here and I am not going to get anything lower than an "A". I'm writing my thoughts down, so what does he want now?

"What is it Mr. T?" asks Patrick with

apprehension.

"Look, Patrick, I think you got a raw deal. But, there is no point in you dwelling on the past. You have a bright future and this will be something that you look back upon and laugh about," replies Mr. T with an assuredness and coolness that has instant disarming effects.

"I'll try to stay cool Mr. T, but this really sucks. I mean, look at the type of kids you have in here. They are really not my type, you know?"

"No, what exactly do you mean Pat?" Mr. T asks with a disturbed look on his face.

"Well, uh-..." Patrick stammers.

"Well uh nothing, Patrick. I know what you mean and I think that this program is just what you need to get you ready for the real world where you can't isolate yourself from the rest of the population. I keep deluding myself into believing that all you kids try to get along, but I am constantly disappointed when kids like you, who are supposed to be the example of how to interrelate, judge people and go back to the type of segregation that occurred fifty years ago."

"I'm sorry Mr. T, I didn't mean it like that."

"Nobody ever means it like that, but the fact of the matter is that you aren't better than your fellow man just because you come from a background where your entire family supports and loves you, and honestly, a lot of these kids don't have that luxury."

Man, Mr. T sure does a quick turn on to your conscience. I never felt so bad in my life. But, he got through to me, which was the point. I hadn't considered those "slackers" and "thugs" and their home lives and stuff like that. Mr. T doesn't play, he just lays it all on the line and makes you think. No wonder so many different types of kids gravitate to his room before and after school. He doesn't discriminate and by God doesn't accept anyone else doing it either. He cares about people and thinks relationships are the basis of successes. I think I will learn a lot from this guy. Jacque was right about him.

Alex Green

Nobody likes me. I have been an outcast since the first grade. If I don't take my medicine, I get really angry and depressed. I have a really hard time dealing with women. My therapist says that has something to do with my relationship with my mother. She takes a lot of stuff out on me and so I guess I don't deal well with women who try to be bossy with me.

Mr. T told me that I need to get my thoughts down about my anger toward women and try to rationalize the reasons that I get so bent out of shape when there are women around me. I know Mr. T cares cuz he was there for me when I first started getting in trouble for yelling at my female teachers and classmates in class. He taught me how to control my anger.

When I was in his class, we set up a system where anytime I felt boxed in or threatened I could just motion toward the door and get myself a drink and a chance to diffuse the time bomb ticking inside of me. Mr. T also helped me out by talking to all of my teachers and explaining to them the system we worked out and I was doing really good until Mrs. Hammond got loud and told the class we were all whiners and slackers. I couldn't get out of the class fast enough to avoid her asking where I was going, so I exploded in her face and that got me an instant referral, which because of the insubordination, got me a free ticket out of her class and into the 3-to-5 program.

I don't know whether Mr. T is too proud of the way things have started out, but that Keisha girl is always making me angry. I hope she follows the contract Mr. T draws up for us. He is always fair and I know that all different kinds of kids listen to him. I've had Keisha in other classes and she never listens to any teacher, but she listens to Mr. T because he doesn't judge anybody.

Patrick seems to be okay, but all the preppies act like that to your face and as soon as you aren't in an isolated place with them (3-to-5 program) they ignore you and treat you like crap.

I kinda look forward to this program because Mr. T always has so many kids around him during the day that I don't get to talk to him too much. I want to talk to him about the poems I am writing. I entered a contest on the internet and I got a reply that says I am a semi-finalist. He looked at my poetry a few years ago and got me convinced that I am good. He wrote a couple of books, so I figure if he thinks I am good, then I have a pretty good shot at getting my poetry published.

As for the letter and requirements for this program, I don't have any problem with all of that. I always work better when I am in a classroom with Mr. T, so I should do fine as long as Keisha and Jamal leave me alone.

Mr. T just received a list of all of the seniors who will be involved in the 3-to-5 program for the rest of the year and it is a helluva combination of kids including: Ricky Terrell, the highly touted, much recruited football stud, Patrick Matthews, the straight "A" student and National Honor Society president, Jamal Lee, the constant comedian, and LaStacia Foster, the actress, cheerleader and track star.

Mr. T says that all of us in the 3-to-5 program this year have to write a letter to the senior class principal, complete a senior class project that is approved by our grade-level administrator, and complete the assigned amount of additional community service hours tacked on to our original requirements.

Also, Mr. T says that those of us who have been completely kicked out of day school or taken out of at least one class have to recover the credits we would have received in those classes, and everyone has to write their thoughts down in a journal daily. It ought to be an interesting year. I hope I can keep myself from snapping anymore. I'm sure Mr. T will help me with my control.

Jamal Lee

I was gonna grad-u-ate and have no problems, but I got high. I was gonna do my detention, but I got high. I would have made it to truancy court, but I was high. Now I am in 3-to-5 and I know why. Why man? Because I got high. They say this is my last chance cuz I been high. I am pretty sure I can get through this, cuz right now I'm high, now I'm high, now I am high. Do do do do do do.

My name is Jamal Lee representin' West Philly, yeah. All the weed I be smokin' is makin' me so smart that I don't need any of this shit-- mother f...!

"Look Jamal, this program is here to help you get your credits, graduate and maybe you will learn something about life in the process. I don't know for sure. What I do know is that this is inappropriate for class. First of all, you are not high right now. I know you like that song and 'AfroMan' is what they call you around here

18

sometimes, but after getting stuck in this program and with just a semester to make up your credits, you better start taking things a little more seriously."

"Damn Mr. T, I forgot how much you can talk. Do you forget to breathe when you get on a roll? I thought you was gonna talk me all the way to 5:00. A'ight, we cool and all, but you can't completely hate on the 'AfroMan', I mean, that shit is funny."

"I'll admit it is a little humorous, but it is definitely not appropriate when you are trying to get out of this place on time. What happened Jamal? Last year, you slacked a little, but you were in all the upper level classes and you did well in all classes except for Calculus, which is understandable."

"I don't know what happened Mr. T. I guess I kind of fell apart after that day when you was pissed at our entire Honors English III class for being such slackers. You went off on the whole Honors Program and you told us that we didn't deserve weighted grades and that they weren't going to make a difference anyway. You said that the colleges wasn't gonna take no weighted grades. I had just been working my ass off for so long and stressin' out so bad over my overload of upper-level courses that I hit my breaking point. You saw me cry in class. I never done that in front of my peers before."

"I remember that Jamal, but you've been

frustrated a million times before. What made this time turn you into a slacker and a full time pot smoker?"

"I don't know man. At first it was all just part of my image—a joke, you know. Then, when I snapped I went from doing it once or twice a month to every day before and after school. They say it ain't a physical addiction, but my mind said I needed to be chiefin' to be happy, so I never stopped. I promise Mr. T, I ain't been chiefin' since I got in trouble for truancy."

"Okay Jamal, but I will be watching you. I've been around long enough to know when a student comes in here high. Don't test me. I hate it when kids don't make it, but that doesn't mean you can take advantage of me either. You know me Jamal. Do your work, write your letter, do the community service, write in your journal and we won't have any issues. You may even have fun in the process. Maybe we'll get back to the old days, find your humor again and stick it to 'em with comedy."

"A'ight Mr. T, whatever. Can I get the rest of my thoughts down so I at least start off doing what I'm sposed to do?"

"Write away AfroMan."

I can never completely read Mr. T. Sometimes I think he my best friend, but then he turns around and disciplines me, but it is never too much and I never notice what he doing until he walks away. Ol' Dude is smooth.

Mr. T is right, I got myself in here and it was because I let myself go. What was I thinking? I really need to step it up now. I don't want to be one of those cats that sit around in their momma's basement getting high and having sex with random girls who are also going nowhere. Those girls get pregnant, and what kind of man would that make me? I ain't ready to be nobody's baby daddy and the world don't need no more dead-beat dads.

From now on, I am gonna try to get back to my old self. I'm gonna stay straight, no marijuana and I am gonna be mad clownin' like the old days. I'll let my performance get back to where it sposed to be in this program Mr. T got going.

Man ever since I quit getting high, I have realized what a stereotypical waste I have been. I was on my way to being a real menace to society. I used to joke around with cats like that, but I wasn't them. Man, I am only a couple of steps from being just like them now. That shit scares me. I'm too smart for that. Bump this, I'm changin', but not before I get high one more time.

LaStacia Foster

Mr. Tompkins told me to write my initial thoughts down, so here they are. I guess they are going to be checking on our journal entries periodically to see how we progress to the real letter.

It is kind of embarrassing how I got in here. I am not a bad kid. My mother thinks I have shamed the entire family, but I just look at it like I made one mistake.

I guess I better get right to what I did, so I can make amends for it ASAP. Well, we were riding on the bus for a band trip and some of us in the back of the bus decided that we ought to play "Truth or Dare", which would seem innocent enough.

I am a flag girl and this was going to be our final Marching Band performance of the year. We were going to perform at the Fiesta Bowl and we were all really excited to be getting to go there.

Gosh, these people in this class are completely rude sometimes. Anyway, I usually wouldn't play a game like this because my mom would kill me, but she likes the boys that were in our group. They have been to our house and they are mixed too. I am Korean, Black and White, and they are some combination like that too. Mom thinks they are good kids. She's Korean and she thinks they are good kids mostly because they are boys and they are cute and they are mixed like me.

We started to play and nobody really noticed but the people in our group. It was one of those things where no one caught us playing the game, but gossip led to us being caught and suspended. For me, it meant I had to end up in this program.

I started the game and took the first dare. All they dared me to do was show my left cheek, which doesn't embarrass me at all. I am proud of my body and it wasn't like it was a boob or something. Anyway, I had on a thong so I just pulled my pants down and showed them both of my cheeks and things just escalated from there. It seemed like we only had dares and no truths.

The guys showed us their penises and a few girls showed their nipples or pubic hair, but I didn't realize it was going to get that graphic, so when they got back to me I said we should quit the game, so we did. I thought all would be forgotten with no harm done.

Well, I was wrong.

The gossip went from one group to the next until this real religious chick heard that people had exposed themselves. As soon as we got home from our trip, she went to her dad and told everything she had heard. But, she said I was the ring leader and that because I am so popular and a dance teamer, actress, flag girl, track athlete and stuff like that, that I caused the whole incident. She didn't even mention anyone else, and I never would narc on my friends. So, here I am. My popular butt is sitting in this seat when I should be at dance team practice. Now I can't be prom queen and that just sucks—Prom queens don't suck, I wouldn't even go there—I meant not being able to be prom queen sucks.

I was given permission to stay in the musical since I am the lead and they didn't want to undercut its success.

And, unlike some of the kids in here, I can't go to day school. My teachers send me my assignments from the classes I was in and Mr. T will hand those in for me, but it isn't as easy as it sounds. I have to complete all of my work during the 3-to-5 program and I can't take anything home to work on. I can read outside of class, but that is it.

It's funny how we stretch the rules for some people some of the time, but not for most people any of the time. I think I could have just been suspended short term if Lurch wouldn't have gotten involved. He doesn't know what race I am, but he probably thinks I am either Black or Asian. Who knows? I had heard that he was harder on those who are not White, but I am White, only I don't look very White, oh well. I'll deal with it, but when I graduate, I wouldn't mind exposing my butt one more time so Lurch could kiss my popular ass! You know, I need to quit referring to my butt like that. People are going to start to get the wrong idea.

Nakeisha

That Gemini character is kinda strange, but he

cool too. I guess he worked out this deal with Mr. T and the administration that we can read to these elementary kids who are in Key Club cuz they don't got no place to go after school. He figgered that we got to do some community service, so he gets us an hour three times a week where we don't gotta do shit but read to these lil' kids.

I can deal with that. Some of these little f... Some of these little kids are cute and my cousins is in here, so it gonna be a'ight.

I've been reading to this kid name Jumar, which is kinda funny cuz he white and he ain't mixed with nothin', but he got a black name. I guess he was adopted by this black family who adopts kids and tries to make a better life for them. That's cool, but I think they shoulda gave him a white name like Matthew, Jarrod, or Jacob.

He be tellin' me the craziest shit I ever heard sometimes though. The other day he axed me if I ever see some ol' dude walkin' round the mall like he ain't got no sense. I tell him I seen him before and he say, do you notice that he carries around a bag and a two liter? I say yeah and shit and he say that that kid name is Johnny and that it's his real brother and that he was adopted by Mr. and Mrs. Walker, but his brother was almost out of the house before they started adopting kids.

He got three adopted sisters and two adopted brothers. Jumar tells me Johnny was born addicted to heroin or some shit and that his real parents used to keep him quiet by giving him whatever drugs they had on hand. So, Johnny is really f... in the head and he got to stay at this retarded house and when he gets free time he goes to the mall cuz most every body in town know him real good and everyone nice to him. 'Cept some time people ask him to dance and stuff cuz he funny to watch and Jumar say that Johnny don't know people making fun of him, but he know and it hurt him real bad to see his brother like that and know that he coulda ended up just like that if the Walkers hadn't adopted him.

Jumar's real mom got caught up recently and she over at Pawnee Mental Health, but I don't know how they gonna cure that f... up bitch. Jumar say his dad move away to some place in California where everyone just sit around and take drugs.

I don't know if Gemini realize we was gonna run into some crazy shit like this, but I think Mr. T knew cuz he paired me up with this little punk and I can't clown on no kid, especially one with that kinda issues and baggage. These kids are all drawn to Gemini though. I guess he been a volunteer for the Key Club kids since he was a seventh grader. You gotta respect a guy for shit like that. I woulda never done nothin' like this if Gemini hadn't got us out of an hour of after school to read to these kids.

I'm glad we don't actually have to read to 'em the whole time. Mr. T give us fifteen minute at the end of class to just talk to the kids and shit. So me and Jumar, we cool and I would do just about anythin' this kid want me to do for him.

Damn Mr. T, I jus' remember how you say you gonna bring out the soft side of me and I wouldn't even realize.

You some shit Mr. T. I can't believe how you tell me you gonna sneak up on me and then you do it. Ain't no one out there ever gets the best of Keisha and get away with it, but you my dawg and that partially why, but damn!

Gemini

It looks as though my community service plan is working quite well. Nakeisha is well-behaved at least three hours a week, which allows the rest of us some peace. I didn't think she and Alex would ever get along, but after her edification via young Mr. Jumar Walker, Nakeisha has had a change of heart toward all those who have "issues and baggage".

I rather enjoy the time spent with the children and it brings out the best in each of our individual characters. I noticed Jamal was having a blast using different voices for the kids and being a complete ham. Ricky Terrell is by far the best reader of the group and his sheer size leaves all of the kids in awe of him.

I won't say that I am surprised by his intelligence level, but he does mask it pretty well a lot of the time. He plays the dumb jock role very well. But, like he says, he gives the people what they want to live vicariously through. If that means that he has to look dumb so that others don't feel bad that he received all of the athletic gifts, then so be it. I could never be something that I am not. Patrick calls me a "unique" and I have to agree that I am exactly that.

Patrick seems to have gotten the chip off of his shoulder as soon as Mr. Tompkins pointed out the self-segregation and condescension Patrick so readily enacts. He is actually having fun with the children and all of his peers, which is good to see. I have always admired his intelligence, but his smug condescending habits were starting to wear on me.

LaStacia seems genuinely concerned about helping the kids learn the importance of reading and role models. She has enlisted two of the young girls in dance camp. And, they are completely enamored by LaStacia's presence.

We were all taken aback by the words of young Mr. Jumar Walker as he drew a crowd by telling his story about his real dad and mom and Johnny. All of us have noticed Johnny in the mall and, actually, the one thing that Johnny has that is similar to young Mr. Jumar Walker is his endearing smile. Johnny is a likable character. A crack head, but a likable character nonetheless.

My job as a tutor is going pretty well. Really, my only client is Mr. Foster who needs help with his Calculus. Otherwise, this group is full of brains. It is like God decided that he wanted our universes to come together in a strange partnership of different personalities, races, range of looks and similar intelligence levels to learn something about ourselves. I believe before this is over we are going to learn plenty about ourselves, but more importantly, we are going to find a way to right the injustices that we have weathered to end up in Mr. Tompkin's modern-day Breakfast Club in the afternoon.

I guess that would make us The Supper Club, but that makes us sound like a masked strip club, or some sort of senior citizen get together club where you get a discount if you bring your card to be punched. Maybe we should go with Nakeisha and call ourselves the 3-to-5 Crew, but that sounds like we all have extended jail time in Topeka. One thing we all have in common is that we all want to get out of here, so maybe our group should be known as Senioritis.

We are what we have. Wait a minute, that could be scary. Some in our group are sexually active. I certainly don't want to be known as the venereal warts.

Our name is Senioritis and we will make it through.

Ricky Terrell

I saw Ms. Brown, my English teacher the

other day in Aggieville. Since I am going to attend nearby Kansas State University on my full-ride scholarship, I frequent the bars there all the time. From the looks of Ms. Brown, she frequents the bars more than I do. She asks if I was doing okay with my assignments and I told her that I was. She asked if she was giving too much homework and I told her that she was.

Ms. Brown started in with me, obviously drunk.

"Ricky, you are a great athlete."

"Thank you, Ms. Brown," I responded, uncomfortable.

"I like the way you move in and crush the quarterback."

"Thanks Ms. Brown."

"Oh Ricky, you know Linda Moore right?"

"Hi Mrs. Moore. Yeah, I had her for Science last year."

I felt like I was at a middle school dance. These ladies were a little too inquisitive and shouldn't they be wondering why I was at a club and drinking too? I am only seventeen. I mean teachers don't have to be perfect, but give me a break. They could at least pretend to care. And, by the way, wasn't Mrs. Moore just dancing with K-State's star quarterback and didn't I see her doing body shots with him earlier? What's up with that? She's married too.

A slow song came on, something by NSYNC, and Ms. Brown asks, "Ricky, do you want to dance?"

"Sure," I sputter nervously.

Okay, I can handle getting mugged by these teachers and I can even ignore that Mrs. Moore is married and doing things that are reprehensible, but what is up with this Mary Kay Letourneau shit? I like Ms. Brown, but not like that. She is way past her prime and the amount of alcohol intake over the last ten years of her life has all gone to her butt, her thighs and her gut. Sick. I don't want any part of this and it looks like she wants one particular part of me.

The part where Ms. Brown begins to grind her ass into my crotch is where things started getting a little weird for me. I wonder where she wants this to go? If it was Mrs. Moore, well that would be a different story. I would love to make her my own personal bopper. Hell, if that's the kind of role model she wants to be, I am willing to give up my standards for that tight and hella fine bootay!

"Do you need a ride home, Ricky? I'll let you drive my car," Ms. Brown says sounding like a naïve little kid.

"I wasn't going to leave for awhile, but a'ight, I'll go with you."

"Great. Linda, we'll see you later."

"Okay Diana, don't do anything I wouldn't do," Linda Moore says as she giggles and plants her head on the chest of K-State's stud QB.

What am I supposed to do now? I am running through all of the possibilities in my head. I mean I have dealt with high school groupies who want to get close to me and ride my coat tails to the pros. But this is an adult and a teacher. One of my teachers to boot. I have slacked a lot in English and I am not passing her class right now.

I drive to my house, in Ms. Brown's Dodge Stratus. I have to admit I feel pretty cool, but I am a little nervous. How will I respond to her when I see her at school? What will my peers think? Ms. Brown just put her hand on my thigh and I have to admit that even though I made fun of her body, there is something about her smile and the power that she has over me that is giving me a major woody.

I haven't really said anything during the drive. It takes about forty minutes to get to my house from Aggieville. Ms. Brown has asked me a million questions which all of my answers have ended up being uh, uh, or uh huh. What a dork I have turned out to be.

Ms. Brown's questions have lessened, but her aggressive nature has not. I began to watch my speed closely because this chick is causing me major sensory overload. She begins to slowly slide her hand up the inside of my thigh and she

32

actually cups me in her hand and runs her fingernails over my crotch. I am not sure how to react, but I hope we get home soon.

As soon as I take exit 299 into Grandview Plaza, Ms. Brown tells me to pull into the church that looks like an old restaurant. I do as she says and park the car. Ms. Brown unzips my jeans and lets me out.

I am too much of a gentleman to tell the rest of the details, but I will say that Ms. Brown gave me a new experience. I guess she is an English teacher because she is a master of linguistics or something like that.

I drove the rest of the way home and Ms. Brown gave me a hug as I walked to my front door. It felt weird, but I felt pretty powerful after that.

"Good luck with the rest of the school year. Things are looking up for you in English. Oh, and good luck with your football scholarship. You are one hell of a...player."

Diana Brown is a master of the English language and I think everything she says has a double meaning. I am not sure what she meant about my English grade, or was she grading something else that had been up? And what did that comment mean about being a hell of a player? Was I a hell of a football player, a game with the girls player, or did she just mean that I played the game the way Diana Brown, the master manipulator, wanted me to play it?

Which reminds me, what was Mrs. Moore thinking. I do feel bad about what I let happen tonight, but the adult was in control, I think. Since Ms. Brown did what she did, does that mean that Mrs. Moore would do that too?

I mean, I feel bad, but I am only a male human species who does only what he can to please the female human species. Especially those with the hella fine bootay like Mrs. Moore.

My question is where was Mr. Moore while Mrs. Moore was playing with the star QB? She used to tell us how in love she and her husband were. Are they really in love, or does she just say that as a front? I know he is gone a lot for his job, but that doesn't excuse her.

I will have no problem excusing myself if I accidentally slip into a hot love-making session with the authority figure Mrs. Moore. I mean she is a science teacher, so as a good student shouldn't I engage in an extra-credit test of our body chemistry? I think me plus her equals HOT BOOTAY 4 ME TO ENJOY!

All I have to say is these women are brave. Junction City is a small Kansas town. Rumors fly quickly, especially when they are as interesting as this one would be. Oh well, I guess that's their problem. I'm just a young man trying to make it in this oppressive world. It's good to be the king.

Patrick Matthews

LaStacia asked me to a party in Westwood, which is a section of Junction City that some consider to be a little rough, but there are lots of nice people there, and I don't see it as being that bad. She is going with me, but I am taking my girlfriend, Jacque with me. It should be fun. We are just going to dance, hang out and have a good time.

We are all having a good time and I just sit back as LaStacia and Jacque talk about me and LaStacia and our new found home in the afternoon. The one common denominator between all of us is Mr. Tompkins. We are all thankful that Mr. Tompkins came to our school. If he wasn't there, our high school experience would be shit. Who else would take up for kids when everyone else doubts them?

Anyway, we are all just chilling and talking to each other when this group of GI's show up. None of us stops what we are doing. GI's frequently show up at our parties. It is no big deal.

LaStacia and Jacque are talking about the musical because that is one thing they have in common, acting. Both have had lead roles in either the play or the musical. They are good and people look up to them. They also have controversy in common. Jacque had to deal with a lot of the rumors that developed over my

35

plagiarism predicament. LaStacia took all the heat from parents after the "Truth or Dare" incident. Parents of honors kids always think their children's shit doesn't stink. Whatever.

So, Jacque Jones and LaStacia Foster are talking about the upcoming musical and these GI's come over and one of them starts yelling at LaStacia.

"LaStacia, what the hell are you doing here? You said you couldn't go out. I thought you had to work? What happened to that bullshit?"

"Listen Ken, you don't own me," LaStacia emphatically states as she backs Ken off with one hand on her hip and the other pointing up and down in his face at the same time.

"I may not own you, but nobody lies to me bitch!"

"Who you callin' a bitch?"

"Hold on here, is it really all that serious, Ken? That is your name? Right?"

"Who is this, little bitch?"

"This is my friend Patrick and you need to watch your mouth!"

"I got you, ho!"

"That's right, get to steppin' Kenneth," LaStacia says at a low roar as Ken is almost to his car.

"Whoa LaStacia, what was that all about?"

"Oh, him? He's just some guy who I dated once. He thinks he owns me. I told him I didn't want to see him anymore and that if I wanted a drill sergeant for a boyfriend, I would join the Army."

"You gotta be careful Stacia," I say in consolation. "Those guys could be dangerous."

"I know. Damn, you sound like my mother."

"Well, maybe you should listen to your mother."

LaStacia's eyes seem to fade into a realization that there is a part of her life that she is not in complete control over.

"Jacque, Patrick, would you guys mind taking me home, I don't feel too good."

Jacque and Patrick instantly turn to helpful caring friend mode and nod their head understanding completely that there is a time for advice and a time to comfort. This was a time for comforting. LaStacia knows she has messed up and she is embarrassed by the scene Kenneth Palmeiro has caused.

"LaStacia, we'll do whatever you need. Let's go," I state with a coolness that has helped me perform at such a high level for such a long time in my stress filled courses.

After dropping LaStacia off, I didn't feel like doing anything, so I dropped Jacque off and she seemed to understand. I am worried about LaStacia, but I don't know that I can do anything for her. I think she is completely on her own on this one.

Okay, this journal is supposed to be part of what we are required to do to get credit for attending the 3-to-5 program. I only have to gain credit for the AP History class that I got in trouble in. So, I feel like I need to spend a lot of my time on the community service and journaling aspect of this program. At least until I get to the part where Mr. Tompkins gives us all the details we need to write our "Why We Are Here, Why We Are Sorry, Et Cetera Letter" to the administration.

Mr. Tompkins talked to me about how I got in here on the first day and we have talked about how what I did was wrong, but the consequence didn't necessarily match the offense. Look, I know copying a paper from the internet is wrong. My classmates knew it too, but we all did it. Why? Because our teacher is young and inexperienced and we thought we could get by with it.

Mr. T says the problem is that younger teachers believe they need to make examples out of other students to make a point. The fact of the matter is I am the perfect student to make an example out of. I am easily the only qualified salutatorian; I was president of National Honor Society and I am relatively popular. Who better to make an example of?

Mr. Tompkins also pointed out that any time a teacher assigns a paper that is worth a large percentage of the grade, to do the assignment right, the teacher has to do his part. In this case that would mean checking note cards, matching quotes with sources and looking at rough drafts. It takes a lot of work, but he pointed out that no shocking plagiarism would pop up for students that went through the checkpoints.

Mr. T added that most experienced teachers would not take the offense to the principal and the NHS leader. The problem is something to be taken care of in class and the student should be given the opportunity to right the wrong, especially in cases where there are no teacher checkpoints. He said, if the assignment is worth a large majority of students' grades, then the teacher must become more actively involved in the assignment.

I made a mistake and I now understand that no matter how wrong the teacher is in the way in which she handled the situation, I am still in the wrong. Mr. T pointed out that I only need to worry about the things that I can control. That basically includes me and my reactions to things. If I don't have control over that, then I don't deserve any rewards for getting by on popularity and reputation.

I believe that salutatorian and president of NHS are definitely secondary to owning up to who I am and becoming a man. That is what Mr. T wants from me and, more importantly, that is what I want for myself.

I feel good about knowing who I am and taking responsibility for my mistakes. I know that I am not perfect and that is the most valuable lesson I could ever learn. I also have learned that acting like I am perfect is worse than thinking I am perfect. Mr. Tompkins called me out on that my first day in 3-to-5. He acted like he was my friend and then proved it to me right away by not lying to me. He didn't condescend, he didn't kiss up and he didn't lie to me.

Those are things that some of my so-called friends have done to me and for me so long that I didn't realize what a pompous ass I had become. Things will be different from here on out. I am slowly becoming a man. My first test will be how I handle the situation with LaStacia. It is a delicate matter. Let's see if I can focus on someone other than me for once.

Alex Green

Life sucks. I haven't been to 3-to-5 for a week. My case worker called Mr. T and explained it to him, but I hate myself for letting Mr. T down.

I always stay out of people's way, but no matter what, somebody always has to enter my world. I've been doing fine. I eat by myself in the lunchroom, I keep my head down in the hallway, I don't react when females say things to me, especially teachers. I have tried really hard to stay out of people's way.

I got beaten up the other day. I am in this class

because I couldn't handle the anxiety of going to school full days knowing that kids are gonna be mean to me and that some teachers will yell and I can't take that. So, I only come to school for 3-to-5 program now for the rest of the year.

I can't wait to get out of this place. Nobody likes me. I have always been an outcast. I try to be nice to people. Life isn't fair.

Okay, I was walking home from school and this girl who I have had a conflict with before just comes up to me and pushes me down. I get up and try to walk around her, but this boy pulls me back down again, hard. I tell them to leave me alone, but they won't. I start getting really angry and I try to remember what Mr. T said about anger management, but I can't remember because I am too nervous and I fill up with anxiety and I freeze.

The boy and the girl just laugh as I start to hyperventilate. They would never bother me like this if they knew how long it takes me to recover. This time it only took me a week, but sometimes I can't even get out of bed for fear of not fitting in, which I never have.

I am a pretty big guy, but when I freeze like I did, I can't do anything and doing something would only make me feel worse. So I stand up and yell, "Leave me alone or I'll get Nakeisha." Both the boy and the girl laugh nervously, but they are scared and they leave me alone. Nakeisha doesn't even like me, but it worked. I thought on my toes and got rid of my problem.

I told Mr. Tompkins about what happened and he said that he would be driving me home from now on and that he would be sure to tell Keisha before she finds out from someone else. If she does find out from someone else that I used her name as defense, Mr. T said that I would understand why those two students got so scared.

I feel good that I found a way to deal with my anxiety, for that situation. Now, if I could find something else to get me through the daily stuff. Mr. Tompkins will help and my therapist will help, but my life still sucks and no kids my age likes me. Someday they will respect me.

I will earn their respect.

"Keisha, listen," Mr. Tompkins said in his most soothing tone.

"Whas up Mr. T, I don't like it when you use that bullshit peer medication voice on me."

"Keisha, Alex was jumped by a couple of kids the other day and he used your name as defense."

"Is that all you was gonna tell me Mr. T? Since when do you think that you know stuff before me? You really think you bad don't you?"

"So, uh, you're not upset?"

"Listen Mr. T, I think Alex an oompa loompa lookin' punk ass motherf..., but I am the only one that can have beef with him."

"You mean, you have become fond of Alex."

"Now Mr. T I didn't say all that, but we all in

42

here for somethin' and I figga we all got at least that much in common. And, as long as we in here, I'm gonna take up for my 3-to-5 Crew. Anybody question that and they gonna get stole on."

"So, you guys are a crew now?"

"Mr. T you know I love ya, but don't start tryin' to put words in my mouf. Is Alex doin' a'ight? I mean I be hearin' how he miss a lot of school sometimes cause people be messin' with him and shit."

"You are such a caring soul Keisha, what would Alex do without you?"

"Fa sho Mr. T, you right. But don't think I don't know you bein' all sarcastic and shit. I ain't dumb Mr. T and remember that you ain't never gonna know nothin' about me before I do. I am the ring leader and don't you ever forget it."

"How could I ever forget that Keisha? Keisha will you do me a favor?"

"What?"

"Will you tell Alex that it is okay for him to use your name if he is ever in that situation again?"

"Fa sho Mr. T, but you better tell his oompa loompa lil' leprechaun ass to not get up in my face no more, or we gonna box."

"That's a deal Keisha. Thank you."

"Fa sho Mr T, you always gonna be my dawg, forever."

"Forever ever?"

"See now Mr. T, just when I think you black you sound like some dumb ass cracka imitator, but you still my dawg."

Jamal Lee

Okay, so this is supposed to be where Jamal is writing his journal entries? I am here to talk to the group, but Mr. T know me and he told the 3-to-5 Crew that if I was gonna be allowed to take up their valuable educational business time, that I had to write in the journal just like everyone else. Oh, I see how you do it. Bet.

Everitt Jackson

I am here for one reason and that to tell you what happened to my dawg Jamal. He was around this weekend and he kept talkin' 'bout how he gonna get high one more time. Well he did and that was Friday. I mean he was gone. But, then on Saturday night he wanted to get drunk, so we did.

We was at this party in "The Wood" or Westwood as it is known by outsiders. Anyway, we was at this party and we was buzzin' a little and Jamal, he sees this girl on the roof of the house. Well, he think she look pretty good, so he go up an try to get the girl's attention. He kept making the ps-s-t sound so she know he interested.

And, since she wasn't nuthin' but a tease, she looked over at him and smiled.

I gotta admit this girl was lookin' pretty good, but we all know she jus' a bopper and Jamal so drunk he don't care. She was wearin' one of those tops where you can see nuthin' but they rack. She has one nice rack too. She kept bendin' over and pickin' up her beer and Jamal jus' walked right up to her and he was about to say somethin'.

I quit watchin' and tried to run my own game. So, I'm spittin' game to this hot lil' freshman and the chick with the rack starts to scream. I run over to see if Jamal was playin' some kind of joke, but he wasn't up on the roof no more. She started screamin' that he fell and I couldn't help but concentrate on her rack jigglin' up and down as she jumped up and down and screamed. She jumped one time too many and put her foot through the roof before I realized that she had said that Jamal fell.

I got a little scared and ran through how I was going to conversate this to his mom when she asked what we done done. I kept thinkin' I would say, "See, what had happen was. . ." which is always how we start out what we sayin' when we trying to get over.

Then I saw him.

Man, it wasn't right. There was a few of the younger guys around him, but mostly it was just him that I saw laying there. Man it was so sure

45

real like all the actors say when someone asks about their experience in the movies. I finally realized that there wasn't nobody doin shit for Jamal, so I yelled that someone got to call the cops and an ambulance, and everyone just started runnin'. I wouldn't have mentioned five-o, but I was scared and didn't know what I was sayin'.

One little dude ran right over Jamal. Lil' dude planted his foot right in his face. I woulda stole on him too, but I was just nervous and shaking and I didn't know what to do.

I go up to where Jamal is and I just shaked and cried and kept tellin' him I know that he gonna be a'ight, but he wasn't responding, so I got real scared and started prayin'.

I felt like one of them dudes that "falls out" in church. I couldn't even understand myself. I musta sounded like I was speaking in tongues or some shit.

I kept tellin' him how he my dawg and the girl he was spittin' game to when he fell was the only one who was still there. She kept sayin' how she was sorry and shit. I didn't care about all that, but when she leaned down to look at Jamal, her chest was right in my face and I could almost see everything. So, I stared and then I came back to reality when I heard the sirens blaring.

I took a few steps back and the girl, Dee Dee, she crouched over top of Jamal and told him how she was real sorry and shit and my stomach felt like it was eating itself up. I noticed that this girl had a thong on and when she bent over you could see her ass, which looked good from where I was standing.

The ambulance lady asked me what had happened and I told her, "See, what had happened was there was some other kids playin' with the frisbie and it went up on the roof. Jamal was trying to get it down."

She actually told me to cut the bullshit, so I told her what really happened. She nodded her head and said something about how she was sorry that this happened to Jamal. She put her arm around my shoulder and looked pretty sad. I told her not to worry, but I knew that something wasn't right.

The ambulance lady looked like those doctor actors on the t.v. when they tryin' to tell someone they got terminal cancer or some shit. I was like, wait a minute lady, you ain't got to put on some sad show for me. I know you ain't concerned about no brother. I guess I had started yelling without realizing it and she just looked down and nodded her head and patted me on the back.

She did let me ride in the ambulance with Jamal. Man, it ain't fair. Jamal wasn't gonna get faded no more. Getting drunk was somethin' we had just always done since we started goin' out to house parties and shit like that. I was real quiet on the way to the hospital, but the way that ambulance lady looked, and the look she gave the driver, made me sick to my stomach.

47

I waited for Jamal to get woke up, and I was there for several hours. The doctor came out to tell me, and his mom who had just shown up, that he would be in a coma for a while.

I was just chillin' with Jamal a few hours before and now he in the ICU. This is f... up and I don't care if everyone in this mug hear me say it. Jamal and me has always been boys and things ain't gonna change just cuz he had a minor setback. Jamal's mom told me it was gonna be a while, and she thought it would be best if I went home and came back on Sunday afternoon.

Well, when I got up there on Sunday afternoon, things ain't gotten much better, but Jamal opened his eyes one time and I was feelin' better. By Sunday night, Jamal was awake and he was talkin'. He say Ev a few times, so I know at least he hadn't made himself retarded by falling off of that roof.

I thought for awhile that he was gonna be brain dead and that scared the shit out of me. I could just imagine all the ass I was going to have to kick if Jamal was some retard.

Motherf...ers will say the stupidest shit when they don't know its your boy they talkin' about. Bump that, I'm just glad that he alive and breathin' and that he knows who he is and he should be able to wipe his own ass. He my boy, but I ain't wiping a brother's ass no matter who he is. Sorry, Ms. Jackson. You raised me better, but dukee ain't my speed.

On Monday morning I showed up in Mr. T's room. There was a few girls in there talkin' to him, but they saw how I looked and they must've figured that I needed Mr. T more than they did at that particular moment.

I told Mr. T what had happened and he just listened like he always do. Then, I started crying and told him Jamal was sorry for what he did. Mr. T is always tellin' us that he wished we didn't do illegal things, but how he knows we do 'em and when he know you real well like me and Jamal, he get real specific about what he talkin' about.

Mr. T said that he knew Jamal didn't want for any of this to happen, and he said he was sorry that I had to experience this. I just started crying like a baby and Mr. T shut the door and told me it was gonna be a'ight.

He didn't say it was gonna be easy, or any flowery shit like that. He just said that it was gonna be okay. He knows that right then wasn't no time to lecture me when I already did what I regretted and regretted what I did.

Mr. T waited for me to calm down and then he told me he thought it would be a good idea if I joined the 3-to-5 Crew, or Senioritis as he says Gemini calls it. I asked him what the point of that would be and he told me to just give it a try.

So, here I am writing in my journal like Mr. T say to and these little elementary kids come in here and one of 'em is looking at me right now.

49

Lil' Dude just staring at my face and his little hand is up on my notebook, which is making it hard for me to write anymore.

Mr. T didn't tell me about this part, but I guess this'll be a'ight. I like lil' kids and shit.

The one thing Mr. T told me extra when I walked in here was that he wants me to talk to these cats in here, and that since I know most of them, and they know Jamal, that he would give me the last thirty minutes of class to tell them what had happened with Jamal. I been in Mr. T's class before during the day and I know that that mean he want us to talk about it and how we feeling and if anyone make fun of anyone else, his ears is gonna turn all red and he gonna look at us like he could kill us or some shit.

I actually kinda like when we used to have those times in class. I don't remember much of the class stuff except how we read this book called Chinese Handcuffs which had a lot of f...-up people in it. I ain't never read no books like that before until Mr. T's class. That kinda stuff make a brother think when he doesn't want to and I know Mr. T get off on that.

The shit that's going on with Jamal remind me of how, in this one short story Mr. T read to us by the same dude, this story character went out and got drunk and drove his boat through this other dude's family's boat and killed almost everyone. That was pretty f...-up and we got into a long discussion about how the dude driving, and the

50

one who lived from the family that got killed in the accident were similar people.

Some pushy chick in that story talked about the universe catching the first ol' dude, but not the one who lost his family and they both did the same stupid shit.

I think that is what Mr. T want me to talk to The Crew for because he expects me to realize that the universe kinda caught up Jamal, and it could get us caught up too if we don't be careful. I'm sure he gonna come up with some unique way to let the whole school know that Jamal need support right now. If he don't come up with something, he'll depend on Gemini to come up with something.

That Gemini's the shit. I mean he kinda look like some geek, but he smart and he not making fun of people who aren't smart like him. And Ol' Dude can dance like nobody I ever see. No one ever say nothing to Gemini cuz we all in awe of his abilities and shit.

Anyway, I guess I'll wrap this journal entry up. Mr. T better be happy. And, it's been harder than hell to write when this lil' dude still lookin' at me, and now he almost in my lap, which reminds me of me when I was a kid. Lil' Dude got my favorite book I used to read when I was little called Fox in Sox.

I kinda look forward to reading that because it's supposed to be a tongue-twister and shit. I never really get tongue-tied when I read that book

though, which is why I want to read it to this lil'
dude. I practice this book all the time cuz I don't
like little kids making fun of me and I got three
little brothers who always asking me to read to
them and they think it's funny when I can't get
through some part.

Lil' Dude got a surprise coming, cuz I nail this
book like I'm flowin' freestyle and ain't no one
gonna make fun of me for that. Cuz, I write
some tight rhymes and I freestyle better than the
best. I'm even better than the really old school
rappers like Doug E. Fresh and Heavy D. They
was supposed to be the shit in their day, but now
Doug E. does old school concerts like Vanilla Ice's
punk ass at small town bars and shit. And Heavy
D used to do that old school show In Living
Color, but now he some jacked up lookin'
counselor on Boston Public. Ain't that the shit?

LaStacia Foster

I feel really bad after what we talked about in
3-to-5 the other day. Everitt came into our group
and we figured he just cussed out Lurch and got
himself in trouble, but it wasn't even like that. He
told us about how Jamal got high and drunk and
fell off the roof, and he told us how Jamal said
this was his last time, and how he thought that
maybe it was really going to be Jamal's last time
because the ambulance lady looked at him like

Jamal was going to die.

We all just sat in silence and Mr. T talked to us a little bit, but mostly he made us talk and tell how we were feeling. Everyone gave their own example of how they had done something just as stupid. Everitt brought up that caught by the universe stuff that Mr. T told us when we were freshmen. Everyone knew what he was talking about, so we all just sat there in silence again and Mr. T looked very stern, but he looked like--I can't explain it.

Well, he looked kind of proud of us. Nakeisha never cries and tears rolled down her face as she threatened everyone and told them not to tell anyone that she been crying, but we all know her and know that she was just dealing with how she felt and she wasn't really threatening us, or we would be scared. We're not stupid. Nakeisha would smash us.

Nakeisha said that she felt really bad because she was supposed to go to the party with Jamal and Ev, but she had to go to the class to try and get her cosmetology license so she could do hair and nails. I guess she had told Jamal that she would smoke a blunt for him and think about the times he was going to be missing because this was his last time getting high. She kept saying she let her dawg down. It really got to her.

Patrick and I both talked about what had happened with the GIs in Westwood and how Jamal said he and Keisha would have our backs next time. I wish he would have been around when it happened.

Enough about that, but at one point or another, everyone cried and no one said anything to, or about anyone in the class because Mr. Tompkins taught us not to do that when we were talking about our feelings when we were freshmen, and no one has forgotten that. Romeo and Juliet we forgot, but not the life lessons.

Alex Green said that even though no one in here may have noticed, Jamal had found the two that beat Alex up and Jamal clowned them in front of the whole school.

We all noticed.

Jamal did this freestyle and he pulled no punches. No one but Alex knew he was going to do that. Alex just sat there and smiled the rest of the time the class talked. No one had ever done that for him before and Nakeisha let him use her name for protection a while back too, so Alex was feeling pretty good.

I had taken Alex out to eat recently because Mr. Tompkins said it would be a nice gesture. Patrick invited him over one night to play Grand Theft Auto and everyone treated him like one of the guys. I don't think Alex thinks everyone hates him anymore.

Ricky Terrell said that he knows the girl that Jamal was staring at when he fell and he would've fallen too if her chest was in his face. He didn't say it in those words, but it meant the same thing.

That made us all laugh and Mr. T likes to end on a positive note, so he had Everitt ask the class to come up with something special we could do for Jamal in the next couple of days, or by the end of the week. Jamal is in pretty bad shape, so he won't be leaving the hospital anytime soon.

Gemini immediately started writing things down and he showed Alex what he had written and Alex just smiled that same smile that had been plastered on his face since he talked about Jamal. Ricky T shared a few of his ideas with Gemini and Gemini said he would see what he could do.

The rest of the week should be interesting. I can't wait to see what Gemini comes up with. I think I am going to tell Ricky what happened since all this stuff has happened. I am afraid to see his response though. I can't tell Patrick; I just can't do it.

Mr. T let us go without any lecture or anything yesterday. He just shook hands with some of us. He did some ghetto handshake thing with some of the kids and he patted a few of us on the back as we left to let us know he cares. We already know he does. I gave him a hug and told him thank you.

He's been there for me plenty of times and I will never forget his kindness. I know he thinks I will forget because I still haven't gotten him a senior picture to go up with the rest of the collage I made for him last year when I was his T.A.. It says "Mr. Tompkin's Family" and has pictures of all the students who have given him pictures.

He is really proud of the collage and always gives me a disappointed look every third day when he realizes that I have not given him a picture yet. But, then he forgives me when he remembers that I made the collage for him in the first place.

I hope Jamal gets better soon. This place is just not the same without him. The kids miss his voices that he always did for them too. That makes it even harder because the kids keep asking about him. I figure eventually we should just tell them what happened to him. It is like what Mr. T always says: "Kids get lied to most of their life. If no one ever steps up and tells them the truth, how are they going to know whom to trust and how to act?"

Nakeisha

Man, the shit that Ev be saying today really made me think. I can't believe my dawg is in the hospital tryin' to hold on to his life. Everything is just so f... up right now. I don't even know how to feel. The only thing that feel right in my life is that I'm going to be a licensed cosmetologist, but my mom says we are moving over to somewhere in Europe sometime in the summer.

I guess I could use the change. Other than that, the only thing that feels right at this moment is that Lil' Dude, Jumar, he make me laugh like no one can since Jamal. It's like he know that Jamal is hurt, so he is picking up the slack for Jamal. He trying to make jokes and shit.

Jumar is kinda putting all of his issues to the side just to make me feel good. Lil' Dude is really making a lasting friend in me. Once you in with Nakeisha, she gonna always be there for you to the end. Mr. T know that and all The Crew here know that and soon Jumar gonna know that too.

Jumar said he wants to go up and see Jamal as soon as he gets better. And, get this: He say that he been talkin' to his crew, the group that come up to see our Crew, and that they gonna make somethin' real nice for Jamal and they gonna read to him when the hospital start allowing visitors and shit.

Lil' Dude made me feel so happy and sad at the same time. So, I been thinkin'. Jumar want so bad to do somethin' for Jamal because things ain't goin' right for him right now. If he is willing to do somethin' for Jamal, then we should do something for him.

I mean this kid got a crack head brother that everyone always makin' fun of and there's gotta be something that we could do for him. I mean I don't think it would have to be much. His brother, Johnny, is just happy that people will notice him. I mean, shit, I raised money for parties at my crib before, so why not raise money for a little something for Johnny and Jumar. And, we could do it in Jamal's name.

I think this shit could really make Jumar's day. And, who knows, maybe I will become famous for my lyrical poetry while we raisin' money. I gotta talk to Gemini about this because I can get the money, but I don't know what to do after I get the money. Gemini will know exactly who to talk to, and he gonna add his own unique twist to everything.

Well, I gotta quit writing for now because I gotta come up with all the plans for our fundraiser. I gotta talk to The Crew too and see what kind of ideas they may have. With this Crew, who knows what gonna happen?

Gemini

Nakeisha mentioned yesterday that we ought to do something in honor of Mr. Jumar Walker. I concur that some sort of gift must be acquired and dedicated in Jumar's honor. He is the epitome of a cool kid. He has all the attributes necessary to bring home the fulfilling monetary contributions. As Nakeisha might say, "He got the skills to pay the bills."

I have been pondering what we might do to honor this young man. Alex mentioned that since his brother is always at the mall, we should do something for Johnny that all the patrons of the mall would be able to recognize as something in honor of him. Johnny frequents every shop in the mall and all of the workers, owners, and patrons who are ever there know Johnny really well.

Ricky Terrell reminded us that Johnny is always carrying around a 2 liter and a bag, so we should try to find something that could involve those things. And, I've been thinking that this could not only add to our overall community service, but that it could also double as our senior class project.

I will have to draw something up so that I can find some loop holes in the wording of the policy regarding senior class projects. I am sure that we can work something out. Mr. T should be able to help. I want to make sure that whatever we decide to do, that it makes Lurch's life miserable and makes ours a lot easier. In fact, I just got a solid idea of what we might do to obliterate the letter to the administration. We may be able to do an all-in-one for that too. This is going to be great!

Not only will we be able to consolidate our responsibilities, but I am pretty sure that I just found the loophole in the race for valedictorian and salutatorian. Patrick will enjoy this. There is no way they can keep us out now!

I did not realize that the revenge factor would be such a gratifying quest for me, but I am always surprising myself. Lurch is going to rue the day that he unfairly disciplined Gemini and each member of Senioritis.

Senioritis is synonymous with the affliction that Lurch is going to have after we let our plans unfold. The Crew is going to like this, and Lurch is going to feel like he has senioritis, which will mean maybe he will want to leave here expeditiously after this year.

I have just acquired a bit of knowledge that points to a conspiracy equal to the recent scandal in the Catholic church. Although schools are hierarchical like the church, I don't think the school district has the same kind of fire power to fight off what we will bring to the table in an attempt to rightfully defame the character of one unsightly administrator—The Lurch—You rang?

Ricky Terrell

I really like this idea that Nakeisha came up with the other day. It will help us get our mind off of Jamal for a while too. We can focus all of our energy on Jumar and Johnny and from what Gemini just talked to me about, Lurch too.

We were talking about how it would be fun to get revenge on Lurch. Gemini was saying that it would work out great if we just had some solid proof of incompetence or some sort of wrongdoing by Lurch or his staff that could be tracked back to Lurch's responsibility.

Anyway, we were sitting there talking and it

hit me. Sometimes I think I am really turning in=
to the "dumb jock" the people want me to be. So,
we were sitting there talking and I said, "Dude, I
know about a little conspiracy that has been going
on for quite a while now."

Gemini asked me what it was and I had no
problem telling him that me and Ms. Brown have
been bumping uglies.

Gemini had this shocked look on his face, but
at the same time he had this evil grin on his face
too. It was kind of scary seeing Gemini looking
like Dr. Evil.

So, we started talking about it. I told him
everything. I haven't written about it for a while,
but more stuff has happened since that first night
in Aggieville. The parking lot of that church was
only the beginning.

The last three weekends in a row I have gone
to Aggieville, entered the same bar, and I have
seen the same group of people. The only change
is that sometimes Mrs. Moore is there and
sometimes she isn't. I figure that that means
sometimes her husband is at home and sometimes
he isn't. It doesn't seem to bother K-State's star
QB one way or the other. He is either with her or
he has his small harem that takes her place.

Anyway, what had started out as an oral exam
for me has turned into an obsession that I
seemingly have no control over. Ms. Brown has
this thing over me now. I mentioned the Mary
Kay Letourneau thing before, but now I truly

understand it. Teachers don't get paid a lot of money, but they have this power over their students that is completely unforeseen.

I know what Ms. Brown is doing is wrong, but I am addicted. I mean, I talk a big game, but I really never had sex before, and I have it whenever I want it now. But, at the same time, Ms. Brown is in complete control and not me. It is weird and wrong and there is no reason for me to stop any time soon except for the fact that it is weird and wrong.

So, when Gemini and I were talking we decided that I was going to have to end this Sexfest. Gemini made sure that I understood that I could still do it a few more times, but that I would need to report the sin to Lurch before it is all over in order to catch him up. See, Lurch loves Ms. Brown and Mrs. Moore because they volunteer for every committee and they work hard. They are good teachers. Terrible role models, but good teachers aside from that.

It will be interesting to see how Lurch reacts. I mean, Gemini obviously thinks that he will be on the White teacher's side and completely dismiss what the Black slacker has to say. I can't wait. In the meantime, I am going to get it while I can. It's wrong, but it feels so right.

First Gemini said I have to come up with proof and make sure there are lots of witnesses. Gemini is letting me borrow his high-tech mini spy camera and tape recorder so I can get the visual and audio I need to seal Ms. Brown's fate. I also called the K-State QB to let him know that I needed a bunch of the players to show up to the bars tonight as a witness of me and Ms. Brown freak dancing before we leave. He doesn't care because Mrs. Moore is just another groupie to him.

In fact, he asked me if I wanted him to record a video for me. I almost said yes, but I am already going to pay for my sins and I don't need to exponentially increase the amount I owe Him for all of this. So, I told him no, but maybe when I am a rookie D-1 player next year he can show me some extra "game film".

So, everything is set up and I am feeling pretty rotten for betraying the woman who is giving me something so private, but I guess she knew what was on the line from the beginning and I just thought I was one lucky bastard, which I am.

Ms. Brown is kind of a freak. I mean it isn't just the dancing or what we do on the way home. She attacks me at the strangest moments and in the strangest places. I got a note to go down to her classroom after 3-to-5 one day and we actually did it right there in the classroom, behind her desk. I think she gets off on the danger aspect, or she aspires to be a White House intern, but whatever it is or was, I liked it for a while. What guy wouldn't?

But, it doesn't feel right anymore and I kind of feel used, which is kind of confusing because isn't it supposed to be the guy using the chick? I don't know, but I think what we are doing is the right thing and I am glad that the end result could benefit way more people than it will hurt.

It is time for the world to feel the wrath of the misnamed misfits and their mischievous, mapped-out mirage that is going to turn into mucked-up mayhem for the marks who mistreated us misfits. In other words, 3-to-5 is going to make our oppressors realize what Senioritis is all about.

Patrick Matthews

I've been trying to do what I said I would and focus more on my friends than myself. I started looking into this thing with LaStacia and that GI, Kenny. Kenny is a prick, but I guess I took my generalizations about GIs too far. I mean he is just one guy, and I unfairly judged the whole group because of Ken Palmeiro. I am trying to avoid being the person Mr. T called me out as on my first day with The Crew, but all changes can't occur overnight.

I actually made a bold move and called Ken Palmeiro to let him know that nobody treats LaStacia like that. And, in hindsight, that was a pretty stupid thing to do. He would have clearly kicked my ass.

So, I called up Kenny and he wasn't there. A buddy from his unit was there and I was pissed so

I didn't ask if it was Kenny. I just started yelling at this guy for being such an ass. Dez, the guy that answered the phone, let me keep screaming until I was finished and then he told me something that changed me.

"Look kid, This isn't Kenny, this is Dez. I agree Kenny's an ass. You know how I know? About a month before that party you went to in Westwood, we were at this GI get together at Fort Riley. We were just hanging out, having a few beers and Kenny comes in with LaStacia. She seemed a little out of it, so I asked Kenny what he was doing. I mean, Kenny is 26 and LaStacia will be turning eighteen in May. Something is wrong with this picture. I mean, a 26-year-old guy dating a girl that is 17-years-old is messed up. The years between the two is not that great, but the life experience differences between a guy his age and a girl her age would be like you dating a third grader."

"Yeah, so what is your point?"

"My point is that I was worried about the girl and I know Kenny really well. So, I just come right out and ask him what he thinks he is doing with this girl. His response was bold, but that's just because he's a jackass and he doesn't think. He said that he just slipped her the date rape drug and that he was bringing her here to show her off before he took her to have his way with her."

My interest level grew and I asked, "What did

you say to that?"

"I told him he's an ass. Then, I went and told some of the guys what he was planning to do, so we decided it was time for a little black ops. We subdued him and took her home. We watched her until she woke up. We didn't know where she lived, so we took her to that church over by the Grandview Plaza exit, just outside of Junction City."

"Weren't you worried that someone might find her there and hurt her?"

"No, man. That's why we left her there. This was a Saturday night party and we know that church pretty well, and the members usually show up real early and they stay all day long. Plus, I called the pastor or reverend, or whatever ahead of time, so he could get there before anyone saw her. Turns out he knows her, so he got there early and took her home."

"Man, I'm sorry I was such a jerk," I whined, begged forgiveness.

"Yeah, well this ain't the first time someone passed judgment on us soldier boys. We are trained to be thick-skinned. Hey kid, take care of LaStacia, she seems like a nice kid. And, let me know if Ken Palmeiro ever comes near you guys again. He has been ordered to stay away from civilians, so we can nail his ass if he doesn't follow protocol. He already pushed the envelope when he showed up in Westwood. Me and the boys made sure that he won't feel like being that stupid again for a while."

"I don't know how to thank you, and I'm sorry that I judged you guys."

"Like I said, just take care of Stacia and the boys will be happy."

"Thanks, Dez."

Dez told me that he and the rest of his unit took care of LaStacia. This whole thing kind of messes up my perception of GIs. It puts the bulk of GIs on the side of the good guys and one particular GI on the shit list. I have to learn to quit prejudging people so much. I guess I can't change overnight, but I'm learning.

I'm not sure how to approach LaStacia about this, and I think I'm going to have to talk to Mr. Tompkins so I can figure out how to help LaStacia heal. At least I did one thing right. I didn't lecture her that night at the Westwood party. I would have a hard time keeping her friendship if I would've lectured.

She obviously had her reasons for lashing out at Ken and not telling us what had happened. I haven't told Jacque yet even though she is my girlfriend. I feel like telling her would be like betraying a trust.

It's weird how on the one hand, telling her would be like betraying a trust, but on the other hand, I won't hesitate in telling Mr. Tompkins. I guess it's because, even though I haven't gone to him for advice very often, everyone in school knows that he knows everybody's business already and he never tells anyone.

He even hears both sides of the story sometimes from people on both sides and he always acts like it is the first time he has ever heard either story. This guy is a gem. I never thought I would be the one going to him for help, but what could it hurt?

"Mr. T, I need to talk to you," Patrick Matthews says nervously.

"Okay Patrick, what's up?" Mr. Tompkins asks as he motions for the girls and the one boy camping out in the room to leave.

"Well, it's about LaStacia."

"Yes, I know LaStacia very well. She was my aide last semester."

"I know Mr. T, but I just need to know you won't say anything to her."

Mr. Tompkins scowls and gives Patrick a look that says, "Who the hell do you think you are talking to?"

"I'm sorry Mr. T," Patrick shakingly adds, adjusting his misjudgment and looking down for a long second.

"That's okay Patrick, but I thought you were going to work on passing judgment on people without having reason to."

"I was. I mean, I am. I came here to tell you something about LaSatacia and how something that happened with her has taught me how to not be so judgmental all the time."

"Okay. The first bell is going to ring soon, so if you have a lot to tell me, you better get to the point. We can only hold off the kids for so long you know."

"I know Mr. T. I mean, yes sir. I mean..."

"Patrick, relax. You don't have to be so nervous."

"I know Mr. T. It's just that I never have gone to an adult for anything before and I don't know how to act. Okay, here goes. LaStacia went to this party a while back at Westwood."

"Yeah, I heard about that."

"Okay, well her ex-boyfriend comes in there calling her a bitch and acting all crazy and she wouldn't tell us what was going on. She was just distant, so we just consoled her and took her home."

"Sounds like a good choice, so what went wrong?"

"Well, I decided that I should do something about it and I called the guy that was harassing her, only it wasn't him. The guy that I talked to said that he and some of his buddies had subdued her ex, Ken Palmeiro, and they had taken her to that church over by Exit 299. They took her there because Ken had given her Rohypnol, or however you say it."

"You mean the date rape drug?"

"Yeah."

"Oh man, did he take advantage?"

69

"No Mr. T, these guys prevented it. They took her to the church, called the pastor and he took her home."

"Oh, thank God."

"Yeah, we gotta do something for those guys in appreciation. But, my problem is I want to be a good friend of Stacia's. I mean I have a girlfriend, but I really like LaStacia."

"It's okay, Pat. You can have a girlfriend and still have a girl that is a friend."

"Yeah, I know that. Mr. T, I'm worried about LaStacia and I don't have enough experience in these matters to know how to console her. Could you do me a favor and find some clever way to bring all of this up to her without letting her know who told you about it?"

"Yes, I think I can find a way to do that."

"Great Mr. T, thank you. I'm sorry I had to bother you like this."

"Patrick, you know I care about LaStacia, why do you think this would be a bother?"

"I don't know. I guess it is because I've never needed an adult before and Miss Becker made me feel like such a fool because of the plagiarism, and well, I guess I just lost trust of teachers because of Miss Becker. But, I knew you would help me out because I've heard everyone talk about you and how you help kids out. It's just that I still have a bad habit of judging first and asking questions later."

"You'll change in time if you want to Patrick."

"Yeah, well I hope so."

I told Mr. Tompkins about LaStacia and it wasn't as bad as I thought it would be. He asked his routine question of all of us today, "Are you doing okay?" Now, after all this time I know why he does that. It's a way to open up the communication lines without being too intrusive. He asks us every day and then when there's something wrong, our body language shows him that there's something there and he pursues it.

He told LaStacia that he wanted to see her after 3-to-5 today and she didn't argue. She looks like she is kind of in a zone today. She actually looks like she did that night in Westwood. I hope Mr. T can make things better. If not, LaStacia may need some professional therapy. Ken could have raped her, and he would have, if the other GIs wouldn't have been there.

Everyone in here is acting strange today. I don't know what Ricky T and Gemini are planning, but they are being all secretive today. Alex still has that grin on his face and Nakeisha and Everitt are working on their lyrics for that fundraiser thing for Jumar.

I heard a rumor the other day that Alex has got a girlfriend. I guess Ricky T knows this girl who has a lot in common with Alex. She's really smart and she reads those fantasy books like Alex and she wants to be a journalist. Alex wants to be a poet or a writer, so they have a lot in common.

Well, they went to the movies and I guess the classic thing happened. They shared a popcorn, their hands met in the popcorn tub, and Wham-O they're in love. Okay, maybe it wasn't exactly like that, but they're hooked up and Alex is feeling less and less isolated every day.

Alex Green

I have no life. Everybody hates me. What is the point?

Not anymore. That is all the past. I am part of a group, or Crew and people like me. I have been diagnosed with a lot of things, but Senioritis is something that I don't ever want to go away. Senioritis has brought me a group to belong to in 3-to-5, a protection device in the use of Nakeisha's name, and I have a girlfriend.

That's right. Alex Green has a girlfriend. She is everything I could ever want in a girl. She is smart, she has the same interests as I do and she is not an outsider. She has her own group. So, now, I inadvertently belong to two groups.

My girlfriend's name is Dee Dee Anderson. Dee Dee is beautiful. She is way better than I thought I would ever get. I guess Ricky T thought about us getting together after he had heard what happened to Jamal. He knows this girl and he said Everitt had a few things wrong about her when he was telling us that story.

72

He knew we would get along because Dee Dee was up on the roof drinking a Coke, not a beer. It's not because she wasn't drinking that he knew we would be a match. I guess Dee Dee likes to do her reading on rooftops. That is where she finds her quiet place. Dee Dee lives in that house that she put her foot through and she was just trying to find a quiet place to read.

Her brothers were having the party and her mom was out trying to find a man like always. Ever since Dee Dee's oldest brother turned 10, Dee Dee's mom has been leaving the kids home alone while she goes out all night.

The reason Dee Dee was standing up is that she had to pee because she drank too much pop; but, that was what was keeping her awake, so she wasn't teasing Jamal by bending over. She was deciding whether to take another drink and finish a few more pages, or get off of the roof and go to the restroom.

It's funny how people's perceptions of things can be so skewed. And, I never thought she would give me the time of day for some obvious reasons that I guess everyone has probably talked about at some point or another. Her big breasts.

Ricky knew that we would get along because he had tried to hit on her before and she wasn't interested. So, Ricky started inquiring why. She told him that they had nothing in common and she began listing her interests. Ricky agreed and his ego remained because he realized it wasn't him, but that Dee Dee is more than she appears to be.

She doesn't care what people say about us as a couple either. And I don't have to use Nakeisha's name anymore because Dee Dee is tough. She is tough mentally and physically. I think I should have gotten Senioritis a lot earlier.

Everitt Jackson

Nakeisha and me got this whole fundraiser thing figured out. The mall got this spot by the Food Court where they always having school concerts and Santa Claus and all sorts of shit. Well, we called the place and figured out how to reserve it. I told 'em what we was doing and they actually ain't gonna make us pay. I was like, "Are you sure?" They said they was sure. In fact, they're going to donate $500. since we're doing something for Johnny.

Things is startin' out better'n I thought they would, so maybe we can do some shit and make a difference. Me and Keisha already made flyers to hang up in the school. I'm gonna hang them during the school day. Keisha said she gonna take some flyers to Manhattan High School too because just as many people in Manhattan know Johnny as do in Junction City. We ain't never done no shit that anybody cared about before, so maybe this is our chance to do something good.

I just been trying to get all this fixed up, but I

haven't forgot Jamal. He my boy and he ain't doing too good. I thought he said my name that one time, but the doctor said he is pretty sure that he didn't. I don't know what I think. I ain't so sad no more, which makes me feel like I got something wrong with me.

I got emotions and shit, but not about Jamal. Not right now anyway. I asked Mr. T if I was some cold-blood ass or something, but he said that I wasn't. Mr. T say he think maybe I am a little bit scared about what could happen to Jamal and that, if he recover, he may not be the same as he was before.

As soon as Mr. T mention that kind of shit, I got a little emotional. Mr. T's like Barbara Walters, finding that piece inside me that nobody visited yet and making me cry. Damn Mr. T, why you gotta do that?

Now I feel a little better, I guess I hadn't shown no emotions yet and Mr. T say that's not healthy. I gotta admit that it felt good to let some of what I am feeling out. It's like I just lifted 10,000 lbs. off of my chest and shoulders. I had been getting this pain in my chest ever since Jamal fell, but now I don't feel anything there. So, I think I did myself some good.

I hope Mr. T ain't getting' the big head over all this. Like, him seeing me cry. Nobody sees me cry and he know it too. I hope he don't think he Yoda or something—"Much to learn you still have."

Yeah, I know who Yoda is. Just cause that some Sci-Fi shit doesn't mean that I ain't seen it. That lil' dude is funny. Jumpin' around like he mad crazy and then walkin' like he an old man again.

Anyway, Keisha and me got some lyrics written and we ready to perform. Wait a minute, now what does he want? Lurch is like the CIA, you don't want him in your grill, but as soon as you turn around, there he is.

"Mr. Tompkins, I need to see you in the hallway, **NOW!**"

Tommy Tompkins steps into the hallway and asks, "What is it?"

"What is the meaning of this?" Mr. Adams asks as he holds out the advertisement of the performance at Manhattan Town Center Mall.

"As you can see, it is an advertisement for a fundraiser."

"Don't be smug with me. You know that it is school policy to have administrator approval before hanging this kind of stuff."

"I did get permission. See the signature on the back of that poster?"

"Who authorized this?"

"Communication is our ally, sir."

"Who **AUTHORIZED** this?" Mr. Adams asks as his ears turn red.

"I believe the kids got permission from Nick Jocular."

"Jocular, he's not an administrator, he's just an administrative assistant."

"I don't make the titles sir, but I'm sure my freshman class would love to know that Nick Jocular is not an administrator. That would save them on a lot of disciplinary detention time."

"Detention, does Jocular even know what that is?"

"Hey sir, it sounds like you and Nick Jocular need to talk this out. I have never had a problem with Mr. Jocular."

"Why would you, you two are just alike?"

"Well, thank you sir, I respect Mr. Jocular. Is that all you wanted to talk to me about?" Tommy Tompkins asks as he points to the poster.

"Yeah, I think that's about it. You know, I'll be watching you Tommy. Shouldn't these kids be getting their educational requirements fulfilled before they start dabbling in nonsense like this?"

"Hey, you're the one that makes such a big deal about community service."

"I don't consider these kids performing as a service to the community. And, why do they care if this retarded drain on society is happy?"

"A drain on society sir? Can I quote you on that? I am pretty sure that our community would love to hear all of your opinions on this very matter. Jumar, the elementry student who sits over there when my kids read to the elementary kids, would be particularly interested in hearing you disrespect his older brother. Would you like me to call him up and tell him to come early today so you can talk to him? I'm sure our special education teachers would like to hear your presentation on all of the drains on society that they produce every year. Are you interested?"

"Tommy, I didn't realize that kid was in your elementary group. But, you don't have to be such a sarcastic jerk about things either. You and Nick Jocular are too much alike."

"I'll be sure to try to be less like Nick and more like you. After all, I don't really like dealing with all these slack asses and drains on society. And, if I have to deal with a retard on top of that, I am going to quit. I want all children to come in here and forget their home lives and just be perfect little clones."

"Tommy, you are pushing it. You know, I could get you for insubordination."

"I certainly did not mean to be insubordinate sir. I guess that I should be happier about you putting down your staff, my students and their relatives. I am definitely sorry about that,"

"Tommy, I'll talk to you later. I'm going to double check on the validity of these posters. You'll be hearing from me."

Tommy Tompkins whispers to himself as Mr. Adams is leaving, "At least let me ring the bell next time before you appear Lurch," he mockingly adds in a deep voice, "You rang?"

I don't know what is going on out there, but

Lurch is trippin' fa sho. I guess he hates Mr. T about as much as we like him. I don't know how Mr. T put up with Ol' Dude without lettin' loose. I woulda stole on Lurch a long time ago if I was Mr. T. But, I also wouldn't put up with the kinds of kids Mr. T do. They bad and he don't care. He just act like they like everybody else. I guess that's why we like him.

Oooh, you can tell Mr. T is pissed. You don't see him frustrated a lot, but that's what's going on with him right now. He frustrated fa sho. I'll just keep writing in this journal cuz I know Mr. T gotta say something about this soon. He always tryin' to hold back, but then he tell us anyway. He feels this obligation to always be honest with us and shit.

I shoulda known Keisha was gonna say something. She talk too much. She my nigga, but, she talk too much.

"Mr. T, what did Lurch say to you? Why you all red and shit. You want The Crew to take care of it for you? Come on Mr. T, we always tellin' you shit. What, are you too good to share with us?"

"Keisha, watch your mouth."

"A'ight Mr. T, dang, just tell us wassup."

"Okay, Keisha. Lur...I mean, Mr. Adams was just checking to see if you guys had gotten administrative approval before hanging those posters."

"That cake dude piss me off. Why he always got to be so nosy. Ol' Dude hate it if we ain't just sittin' there saying, 'Yes Mr. Adams, we understand.' He a mark. Bump this, I'm going down right now to talk to him."

"Nakeisha! Calm down. I took care of it. I blamed it all on Mr. Jocular and that will definitely keep him busy for a while."

"Ah, Mr. T that's dirty. Mr. Jocular's your boy. How you gonna play him like that?"

"Well, Nakeisha, I figure that Mr. Jocular will handle things fine. He always does. Plus, the freshman class is good this year, so he needs more to do."

"You dirty Mr. T, but I got you. I see what you're doing. You and Mr. Jocular gonna have a good laugh over this one."

"Nakeisha, the good thing about all of this is that Mr. Adams knows what you are doing now and he won't do anything to get in the way because that would be a bad move for him politically. Ever since Mr. Arnold left a few years back and Mr. Adams took over, Mr. Adams has had a really hard time trying to look good in the eyes of the public. Mr. Arnold never had any trouble with that, but he also didn't make that big of a deal about it either. Mr. Adams wasn't prepared for that part of the job."

"So you saying that Mr. Adams is going to crack under pressure. I got you, Mr. T. You're meaner than you look. You should be ashamed

Mr. T. You shouldn't wish bad things on your boss."

"You are lecturing me, Nakeisha? That's pretty funny, but now we need to focus on making sure we get all of this fundraiser stuff done without a hitch."

"A'ight Mr. T, we'll get it done right."

"Can I see your lyrics, I want to make sure that no one holds anything against you guys. Gemini, Ricky, Alex, how is the final plan going? Is the mall going to give you guys what you wanted for Johnny?"

Gemini responds with a tone of seriousness, "Mr. T, everything is in order. We are good-to-go. I hope that Jumar will enjoy what we are planning for his brother. We are going to have him give the presentation after we have secured all of the funds that we need."

"I've checked with Jumar's parents and they said that they are okay with his involvement in all of this," Ricky chimes in.

"Dee Dee and I are designing the picture plaque and I am writing the caption," Alex enthusiastically responds.

"Okay, less talk, more action. The kids will be here soon, so you guys need to get as much done as you can before they get here. In order for us to get everything done on time, you guys are going to have to do some work at home," demands Tommy Tompkins.

It's kinda funny that Mr. T argues with Ol'

Dude about stuff. I mean, Mr. T ain't the one arguing, but Ol' Dude don't realize that he always looks stupid and he just makes us like Mr. T even more. Lurch isn't very experienced with human relationships. Mr. T is though. Mr. T used to teach English when we was freshmen, but now he teaches Life Skills Communications because he unintentionally spent more time with issues in that curriculum than he did with English.

Nobody paid any atttention to nothing but the life lessons anyway. So I'm glad Mr. T changed subjects, but he shoulda done it sooner. If it weren't for the circumstances that caused me to agree to hang out with these kids until the year is over, I wouldn't have had the chance to learn from Mr. T again.

Something is goin' on with LaStacia. She just hasn't been herself lately. I dunno what it is, but she just ain't herself.

LaStacia Foster

I've been thinking a lot lately and I think it is time to reevaluate my life. I had everything going for me, but now it seems like all the obstacles I have in my life are placed there by me. First, there is this Ken Palmeiro situation.

I know Ken is a jerk, but something about him makes me feel sorry for him. I am drawn to him. He always says he is sorry. I don't know. I hope that I haven't turned into a cliché. I am the first person to jump to conclusions about women who are taken advantage of by some sick controlling man. I always thought I was too strong for that.

I guess I am not. The easiest way for me to explain it is to say that I feel an attachment to Ken. I truly thought I loved him. He provided me with a security that most men don't. He has a job, he is tough, and he tells me over and over how much he loves me. When he gets stationed in Oklahoma, he says he wants me to go with him and go to college down there.

I hate to admit that I have considered doing it, but the truth is that I have considered it and I am willing to go there for him. I know that he tried to speed up the process of sex with me, but I was planning on having sex with him anyway. It was just a matter of time.

Ken took me to this GI party at Fort Riley and he slipped me a roofie. I thought that I felt a little strange, but I was really out of it. The next thing I knew, I was at the church and Pastor was telling me things were going to be okay. He took me home, I showered and went to church and started the next week like nothing happened.

This guy, Dez, tried to call and check on me several times, but I didn't want to talk to anyone, so I didn't answer the phone. He is pretty persistent. He kept calling and about a week ago I accepted his call. My mom screens my calls at home.

She likes Ken. She always makes me talk to him. My mom hasn't had much luck in the love department and I don't think that she is a very good role model for me, either.

My dad used her for the money from her good job at the bank and he still doesn't pay what he owes. She lets him walk on her to this day. Getting divorced just meant that Dad doesn't have to answer to Mom about where he has been and what he has been doing.

He still receives the benefits from Mom's check and he never pays child support. I love him, but he is a jerk. And, I am a smart girl. I know that I love Ken just like I love my dad. And, I also know that I love Ken like how Mom loves Dad. It is sick and it is wrong and I need help to change. Ken could ruin my life if I am stuck with him for the rest of it.

Anyway, Dez called about a week ago and asked how things went after I got home from church and if Ken had been bothering me. I told him that I have talked to Ken several times and he responded with a long silence. I asked him what was wrong and he asked me one more time how I was doing.

I explained to him that Ken said that he was sorry and that he had made a bad judgment, but that he would never do it again and that he would make it up to me.

Dez wished me the best and said nothing more. I can't explain it, but Dez's silence was eerie. He seemed to be thinking a lot more than what he was saying. It bothered me a little. The weird part is that Dez seemed to be a lot more sincere in his concern than Ken ever has been.

All I know is that I need help and I haven't gone through my normal channels. I usually tell Mr. T about stuff like this, but he knows this guy called me a bitch before, and that is one thing that Mr. T doesn't tolerate, men who abuse women in any form. Mr. T, Mr. Jocular and Mr. Spence, have all dealt with abusive men first hand and they are not forgiving when it comes to that topic. That is why I have avoided Mr. T on this issue. But, if I know him like I think I know him, he already knows a whole lot more than what he is letting on.

Sometimes I talk to Ms. Santiago about women issues, but she is all about women empowerment and she thinks I am a strong woman. I don't ever want her opinion of me to change. I won't talk to her about this. This is too personal and complicated to tell my friends, so I guess I will have to tell Mr. Tompkins. I always do eventually anyway.

I don't even know why I started writing any of this down. Oh yeah, Mr. T says he wants to see me today after 3-to-5, which makes me think, like I said before, that he already knows something. I am really confused and I feel like I am at the point where I could mess up my life really badly if I go strictly on emotion in my upcoming decisions. And, like I said, I've always let Mr. T help me before.

I really need him right now more than ever. I hope he doesn't think I seem desperate. If he did, he would never show it. I guess that is what keeps drawing me back. My only caution flag right now is that this has to do with manipulation of me by a male and Mr. T is calm and patient about everything but that. I mean, if you want to make him snap, speak in a degrading way about his female students past or present and you will see the shortest fuse on record.

I am really nervous and it is going to be hard for me to concentrate today. I have so many things on my mind right now. The musical is three weeks away and I don't know all of my lines like I usually do. That would normally be okay, but I am the lead this year.

What is really bothering me is that I am a few days late on my period and Ken is the only guy that I have had sex with. He apologized to me several times after the roofie incident and then last weekend we went out one night, had dinner, he brought me flowers and we did it by the water out at Milford Lake. It was a beautiful night and I thought that my whole life could be like this if I stay with Ken.

As soon as we were going to do it, I stopped him and asked him to use protection since my mom wouldn't let me go on birth control pills, and the whole school thinks you have AIDS if you go to the Junction City Youth Clinic across from the school to get stuff like that. So, he puts on a condom and as soon as we start it breaks.

I tell him I want him to be the one. I tell him I want it to be special. He holds me close and tells me he loves me. I begin to feel free and I tell him I love him too. The heat began to swelter around my entire body and I got chills as he began to kiss me softly.

Then, he tells me that if he is the special one that we shouldn't use protection. I know that we should. All of my instincts say that we should use protection. But, I give in. Just like that, I give in. It feels so right and he seems so into me and in love. I know he is sorry for how it almost happened before, and I know he loves me.

Up until that point, it is one of the greatest memories I have ever had. This isn't my first time. I experimented with Josh Robinson in ninth grade and he broke my hymen, so this doesn't hurt like that did. I am completely caught up in the moment until, right at the moment of climax, Ken says, "You wanna get f...? You wanna f... with me? There it is bitch. You f...bitch! How do you like me now? You can take that as the last time I will ever get near you bitch! So you know Dez, huh? Is he your knight in shining armor? I got kicked out of the God damn army because of you. Dez and the boys broke a few of my ribs first. You are a real bitch. Telling me you love me, but telling Dez that we have been seeing each other. The army is all that I have. It's all that I had. You bitch! You motherf...bitch!"

I feel so helpless. I feel like I always have to please this guy. He has such a hold on me. And now he knows me in the deepest of senses and I don't know how to react. I told him I was sorry and I love him and that we'll figure things out.

Am I stupid? I know he loves me, but I watch Oprah, I know that most women are pleasers and the only thing that holds them back is their desire to please their man at all costs. He treated me so nice, though. I know I can change him, but I know that I have always made fun of how weak women who say that very thing are. I can't change him. His personality has taken all these 26 years to develop and I have no chance to change him now.

But, he is the possible father of my possible child. Shouldn't my child have a father? But, I know, on the other hand, that there is a huge difference between a sperm donor and a daddy. Ken doesn't seem like he would be a good daddy. All of my instincts say he wouldn't be. But my heart betrays me. My heart sees Ken at the moments when he is able to be soft and gentle. I have to make myself see that it is the fact that he can be dangerous and scary that should give me the answer I seek.

I am a smart girl and he is a dangerous, sick man who needs help. I am just a kid. He should be a couple of years into a career now, but he is trying to steal the heart away from an eighteen-year-old little girl. I know that is what Mr. Tompkins will say. I am smart enough to avoid this situation, but I let him have sex with me and only one other guy has even come close to that. After Josh broke my hymen, I was in pain and bleeding and there was no joy in it.

It scared me and it kept me away from all things sexual until now. And this time, it felt right. Ken is experienced. But, maybe that is what should scare me about him: That he is experienced. I am just a little girl. That Rohypnol trick was something a kid could be excused for, not an adult. Even a kid would so be wrong for trying something like that. But Ken should have known even better.

Maybe he did.

I don't know. All I know is that I have thought myself into a stupor and I hope Mr. T can pull me out of this funk. I want my life back. My simple, stressed over school and homework and extra-curricular activities that are related to school—kid stuff. I am just a kid. But I am a smart girl. Why do I continue to let these things happen to me?

Ken Palmeiro has penetrated every aspect of my being and I have let him in too close to my soul. I opened up to him and no matter how repulsive he is acting, I can't seem to push him away.

After he screamed at me that night, he drove

off, leaving me lying next to the water with the aftermath of what we had done dripping down my being. I had never felt so used, but sadly, just like those women I have always hated, I feel a strange unhealthy attraction to the man who has left me like this.

I had no idea how I was going to get home, but then I remembered that Patrick and Jacque were going to camp out, so I went to Curtis Creek, Campground D, where their families usually camp and I asked them for a ride home. Patrick asked me a thousand times if I was all right and I told him that I was. He is such a sweetheart.

You see, right there is the type of man I should be drawn too, but instead I am a cliché. I am a stereotypical weak woman who is drawn to the bad boy. The problem with my bad boy is that what makes him bad is not his appearance. He is always clean-shaven and dresses very nicely. What makes Ken a bad boy is that he is a delinquent who would probably be in jail if it weren't for the army and his buddies.

I have already made a huge list of all the reasons Ken is wrong for me. I have also made a short list, in my mind, of all the ways that he is right for me.

I am a smart girl. When the list for why someone is right for you is hardly noticeable, but the list for how they are wrong for you is larger than the list of accolades you have achieved as a highly successful student, something is seriously wrong with that picture.

Well, I haven't gotten much accomplished today, but I will get extra points for my journal. I think I have almost convinced myself of what I need to do. Maybe Mr. T will control his emotions and say just the right combination of things to make me leave Ken Palmeiro and men like him for good.

I wonder if Mr. T feels stressed from all the weight we put on his judgment sometimes. I know he knows we respect him, but does he know that we expect so much from him, so much of the time? If he does and he stays in his profession regardless, he is way more dedicated than I would ever be with that kind of pressure. I should tell Lurch Mr. T deserves a raise.

No, he would probably just hate Mr. T more if I did that. I remember once I told Lurch that Mr. T was my favorite teacher and Lurch asked if I only like the teachers who are easy. And, then he just laughed. It pissed me off and I told him that he may think Mr. T is easy, but whatever we learn in Mr. T's class, we learn forever. How many teachers can you say that about?

Lurch just laughed and said, so you agree with me? Guys like him just don't get it, so I smiled and walked away.

Well class is over. I guess now is the time. Actually, writing all of this down has been kind of therapeutic for me. I don't feel so apprehensive about talking to Mr. T now. Mr. T looks worn out today. Nakeisha has been feeding him some line about her ruling the school again. I just hope he has enough energy to help me make that next step. He has already told me he doesn't approve of Ken. He has this problem with any guy that old wanting to be with a girl my age.

I guess he sees it as perverted. He already told me to look at it like I am dating a 10-year-old. The amount of maturity difference is about the same either way. I tried to argue with him about that, but he immediately said that the analogy doesn't hold true when both people are starting their careers. Then, he said, eight years may seem like nothing.

"LaStacia, are you doing okay?" Mr. T asks in his usual measuring way.

"I'm fine Mr. T. Why do you ask?" LaStacia innocently responds.

"Well, you just look like you are all alone today. You are usually so full of confidence and vigor, but today, you look like Alex used to look every day before he found a group to belong to and a girlfriend. It's just not like you to show externally how you are feeling on the inside."

"Mr. T, I am not even going to play with you. I assume that you already know some of what is wrong with me and I'm not going to ask how. You are right, I need to talk, so no matter how you found that out, I am glad that you brought it up so I don't have to."

"LaStacia, I worry about you. I know that you were seeing that GI and you know what I think about that already. And, now you seem so depressed and I have been afraid to approach you just because I don't want you to completely shut me out."

"So, why did you ask to see me today?"

"Well, actually, I needed you to do me a favor."

"What favor?"

"Well, I was hoping you could be the choreographer of the whole event in honor of Johnny. I know Nakeisha is talented, but she doesn't plan well and you have seen my organizational skills."

"Mr. T, you're right. I should have volunteered when they brought up the idea about this performance. I can have an introduction set up, we can have some of our forensics kids do their humorous solos and we can follow Keisha and Everitt with Gemini and Ricky dancing. That way everyone can be involved. Okay Mr. T, I'll get to work on all of this right away. See you later."

"Okay LaStacia, see you la...Hey, wait a minute. You are smart, girl. You knew that I was tired today and you saw your opening and tried to get out. Now, what is this about you needing to talk and assuming I already know something about this? Do you guys really think I am Yoda and the force tells me stuff?"

"Much to learn you still have, Mr. T."

"My sentiments, exactly. Now, what is going on."

"Well, like I said, I know you know a little of this already, and I know how you feel about older guys preying on high school girls. And, I know that you know I am a smart girl," LaStacia says as she breaks into sobs. "But, I-I-I I am not very strong. I am a rug for men to walk on. I am weak. I am a stereotypical battered woman. I am everything that I always wanted to avoid being. **I AM WHAT I DESPISE.** I am easily taken advantage of. I am overly sensitive. I give my heart away too easily. I want to believe in everything that can destroy me. I am nothing. I am worthless. I am a slut."

"LaStacia, slow down, slow down. What is all of this about? Like you said earlier, I know you are a smart girl. I have faith that you will make the right decision in the end of whatever is going on. Part of being a strong woman is realizing when a man takes advantage of you. You have already done that. The next step is admitting to yourself that you let it happen, but you don't want it to happen again. I believe you have done that too. Next, you have to ask someone you trust to reiterate what you already know to be true. That includes telling yourself that you don't need a man like the one you describe. It includes me affirming that you can be strong, and then you can move on. You have done that.

"The most important thing now is for you to look inside of yourself for the strength to make the decision that will help you move your life forward. I can be here for support if you start to doubt yourself, but I can't make the decision to change your life for you. You have to make that decision for yourself. You have to own it. You can't do this alone. Part of being strong is having the strength to seek the help of all who you are strong for in their times of weakness. This is that time for you. I told you I will be right here to support you, but don't shut your friends out. True friends will help you through your weakest moments.

"Don't be afraid to test your friends. They won't disappoint you. And, if a few do, you can figure that out now instead of later. I am the first friend to say that I will be there to do whatever you need. Now, give some of your other friends that opportunity. You are a smart girl, so you know you can't do this alone. If you try to, you will become weakened by emotions that you have no control over.

"I am sure you haven't told me everything. But, I don't want you to. You know me. You know how I might react if I knew everything. But, I can tell by what you did vaguely say that someone has done you wrong, a man, and you feel lowly and worthless and even slutty, but I know you are none of those things. Your friends know you are none of those things and you know that you are none of those things.

"So, use us now. It is your turn. You have done things for me when I was in need. You babysat for my nieces when no one else would take on that kind of situation and you never asked any questions. I love you, your friends love you, and in time you will love yourself again."

LaStacia cries uncontrollably and she can't look at Mr. T, so he hugs her and just lets her get it out.

Nakeisha

Mr. T keeps hounding me about my lyrics. Damn, Mr. T, I'm gonna get it all done. Everything gonna be a'ight. LaStacia gonna help us fix the show up some. She gonna give us an opening and closing act and she gonna make the presentation with Jumar to Johnny. So, I'm feeling pretty good.

I been talkin' to Ricky and Gemini though, and some crazy shit been happenin' around here. I like to make up shit to make people look bad sometime, but I ain't done that since Mr. T made me sign the contract when I started 3-to-5. But, I never could have thought up some of the shit that Ricky be tellin' us about Ms. Brown.

I had me a "D" in that class, but I'm about to get that shit bumped up. I don't care what nobody say, I am going to get mines. This place gonna give me what it owe me one way or another.

Ricky be sayin' that Ms. Brown actin' like she his White House intern and shit. She be givin' it up for Mr. NFL and he be tellin' it all. He tell us how she attack him at the church after he drove her car home form the Aggieville. She is some nasty shit.

I knew she be thinkin' about them big boys and all, but she likes this negro fa sho now. Hood rat, hood rat. It just like some white girl to be all pure in what she say and then she be doin' all sorts of shit behind closed car doors. Ha ha. She a bopper fa sho. I knew she be given me grades for some reason. She givin' me a "C" and I ain't done shit all year.

But, I bet she do that cuz she think that I know everything already. Cuz, I usually know the gossip and shit. The funniest one that Gemini and Ricky told was on that Mrs. Moore. She be acting purer than God. She sponsor a Christian group here and always talkin' about how much she love her husband and shit. Whatever man, I heard the other day she start sayin' all this shit to her class about how he's abusive and shit.

Yeah, right. He probably just found out about her K-State QB pimp who showin' her where it at. She ain't never had nothin' like that in her life before, so now her husband don't seem all that cool. But, she ain't too cool about how she play this thing off. We ain't dumb. One minute he the coolest thing and then the next minute he be abusive, but there ain't no signs of abuse.

That be all around the same time we hear this shit about Mrs. Moore and Mr. All-American. Give me a break. Have you ever heard her talk about K-State football? It's a dead giveaway. I mean, Mr. Moore was on a co-ed softball team with Ol' Dude and Mrs. Moore play too.

Mr. All-America forgot to bring his glove, so Mrs. Moore play that shit for all it worth and let him borrow hers. She come to class the next week talkin' about how he sweat in her glove and now their sweat is mixing and that make her so excited.

She wrong. You can tell she wrong and now she try to make Mr. Moore look like the bad guy. The only thing he do wrong is that he too nice and he let all this shit happen right in front of his face. I hear she be all over Mr. All-America, but she tell her husband that she is just awestruck or some shit.

Keisha smarter than that and now I know some shit. Ain't no way I ain't passin'. Nobody get Keisha when she can get them first. Believe that. I'm gonna get these boppers. And, I'm smart too. I'll do it just when they think they got me.

Just like I used to do with the race card. Right when I know I'm gonna get in trouble, I say racism and some other shit and all of the sudden, no one has any problems with me and I get my fifth second chance.

These adults around here gonna be sayin' my name for a long time. We ain't lettin' none of this shit go.   And, if Lurch sorry ass don't do something about all this shit, I'm gonna nail his ass too.   Gonna do it for Mr. T.

That'll teach Lurch to f...with the 3-to-5 Crew. He gonna know real quick what Senioritis is all about.   I gonna get him for Mr. T's boy, Mr. Jocular, too.   They the only two adults know how to be fair around here, so I ain't never tried to get over on them and I never will.   But, I'll take up for them and even though I got over on Lurch a thousand time, he mess with Mr. T and his boy, so now that I have a chance for revenge, I'm gonna get it.

Lurch ain't gonna be rulin' nothin' after we get thru with him.   I dunno who they think run this school, but in case they forgot, it's me.

Nakeisha run the school and them boppers and the Grand Wizard Lurch are gonna realize that just cuz they grown don't mean that give them the right to act a fool all the time and make us think that they all perfect and holier than we is and shit. This is too good.   I can't let this shit go.   I try to make up shit that is this good.   What Mr. T used to say about the truth and it being stranger than what you try and make up, that all be true.   He told us that after readin' some novel, but I can't remember what it was.

Everything he teach us come back eventually.

Gemini

I have all sorts of different devious ways to catch up with the deviant acts of our esteemed educators. The one I have been telling Ricky about is my little spy camera gadget.

I feel like the computer guru on Alias.

I have a lot of different devices. I like to play with electronics. I have an unquenchable desire for all things tech-oriented. For Ricky, I have been thinking about a camera that would fit his image.

I have this mini-camera that looks through the tiniest hole in a cellular phone. This mini-camera delivers an outstanding camcorder quality picture with the hi-resolution chip it uses. I believe this will be perfect for Ricky.

I have the transmitters and receivers necessary for this to work great wirelessly at a long range. That way I can record all of the film taken during his upcoming adventures. I am sure I do not ever want to view these seedy videos. They are purely evidentiary and they are going to be used solely to incriminate and serve as proof.

This is going to be the most memorable imprint of sinful indulgence in inappropriate fornication ever witnessed, recorded and ear marked as fodder for the precocious Ricky and his perverted professor.

Ricky Terrell

I wasn't completely sure about this spy stuff. I couldn't believe that anything could be recorded from a cell phone, but Gemini said it could be done, and it looks like everything worked. We'll just see what happens next. I am going to miss the sex, but some things are just meant to end.

The plan was to meet up with Diana at Milford Lake at around 10:00 pm on Saturday night. Ms. Brown showed up a little bit drunk. She is always drunk on the weekends. Anyway, she shows up and is ready for action as soon as she sees me. I used to feel uncomfortable with this. But, once something becomes an everyday experience, the novelty wears off.

Plus, I knew that this would be my last time with her. I am still male and the thought of losing an easy score is painful. I really have no other attachment to Ms. Brown other than that. We have nothing in common. She is still pretty bitchy at school and in general.

As soon as she saw me she was ready to go. I had the cell phone attached to my belt and what the camera didn't pick up visually, it picked up on the audio. This spy stuff is amazing.

Well, Ms. Brown certainly put on a show for the camera she didn't know existed. For a brief moment I was actually concerned about the ethics of taping a professor in precarious predicament with a popular pupil. I think Gemini has rubbed off on me with the alliteration lingo.

How could I worry about ethics when Ms. Brown has all of the power? I soon forgot about ethics as Ms. Brown was feeling on my package. This lady has no shame. She wants me and she is going to have me.

I made sure to talk about what we were doing a little more and made her become more outwardly demanding, which she had absolutely no problem with. I was trying to get the best combo of audio and visual possible since this was my last hurrah. As soon as she got what she wanted, she was out of there like a light.

The most incriminating part of this little episode was obviously the actual sex. The most damning part of the whole deal was Ms. Brown saying, "School's out," when she finished with me.

I, of course, knowing we were being taped asked, "What is my grade?"

She responded with, "You have a "D". You will have to work a little harder for a better grade. You haven't been returning all of the assignments that I have given to Mr. Tompkins. You are on the border line. The sex was an "A", and if you continue to satisfy that requirement, I will average the two scores together. Don't blow it."

Talk about bad timing for her. I considered the offer for a second and then remembered that the goal was to have ammunition to go up against Lurch. I think that to some extent, consensual sex is what we were doing. But, as soon as Ms. Brown brought the school issues into the picture, I think we have a little bit of a different situation—conflict of interest.

My K-State QB buddy pulled through for me too. He had a mini-cam in his baseball hat and Mrs. Moore was all over him. She isn't breaking any school rules by doing this, but she is not doing her marital vows justice. I think that her position as Christian Youth Group sponsor should be in question after this. I guess it all depends on what denomination you are.

Ironically, Ms. Brown is Catholic. Maybe that is why she likes the mentor-student relationship. It makes sense in my mind anyway. Mrs. Moore is Methodist or something. I wonder if Methodists are for extra-marital affairs. I doubt it.

I think that we have enough to make Lurch squirm a little bit. Well, not just Lurch, but maybe the dynamic deviant duo of Brown and Moore. I think that is what Diana thinks of me—brown and more. Anyway, I don't feel extremely comfortable with all of this, but it should serve its purpose.

Gemini says that we have to move on this fast to see what the reaction is for optimum effect. I don't know what he means by all of this, but he sure has an evil smile on his face these days. I can't wait to see how all of this plays out.

Some of The Crew has talked this out and this

is what we are going to do: We are going to have LaStacia tell Lurch that she saw me and Diana in her room making questionable contact. LaStacia is our actress and as soon as we told her what we were planning, she became instantly interested. She said it would help her concentrate on something other than her relationship woes or something like that.

So, LaStacia is the beginning of the plan. We don't necessarily want to get the teachers in trouble, but they can help us move forward to what we really want. LaStacia seems ready and willing to go, so tomorrow, during the day LaStacia is going to tell Lurch what she has seen.

I am setting up contact with the counselors, so that there is proof of my questionable mental status after being taken advantage of by an adult leader. Nakeisha is going to get Ms. Brown and Mrs. Moore noticed a little bit by making comments to them as she passes to go to 3-to-5.

Hopefully everything will work together smoothly to give us the desired end results. We have big plans for these people and this place. Senioritis is almost as dangerous as PMS. Look out because we have a plan with Dr. Evil at the controls, evidence to back ourselves up, Nakeisha to add fuel to the fire, and Lurch to make his predictable moves to protect his prized professors. Perfect.

Patrick Matthews

Things have gotten pretty weird around here lately. Nakeisha got written up by two teachers yesterday and she isn't even in day school. I guess she made some comments under her breath as she walked past Ms. Brown and Mrs. Moore. They got angry and stopped Nakeisha and got in her face. They were yelling at her and telling her they were writing her up for disrespect.

It takes a lot to get those two that mad. There is no telling what she said to them. All I know is that Nakeisha got a two day vacation from 3-to-5 and she has to walk a certain route to Mr. T's classroom so that she doesn't pass by Ms. Brown or Mrs. Moore. Ms. Brown tried to get Keisha kicked out of school, but it didn't happen.

I can't wait until Keisha gets back on Friday. I am sure she has some stories to tell. We won't get anything done. In addition to Keisha getting in trouble, things have been strange with Ricky and LaStacia too. They keep getting called down to the counselor's office and the school psychologist has been here poking her head in frequently to talk to LaStacia, Ricky and Mr. Tompkins.

I am not sure what is happening, but it is going to be guaranteed interesting around here for a while.

LaStacia and I have been talking a lot lately. I think she is on the road to healing. She hasn't seen Ken since he took her out to the lake a while back. She hasn't told me everything about that yet, but I get the feeling that Ken really did something bad. I can sense some sort of abuse.

Anyway, we've been talking a lot and she is seemingly letting me back into her life. I really like LaStacia. It's weird. I have a girlfriend, but LaStacia gets me in a different way. She is my friend, but she is also a connection like none I have ever felt before. She is like a soul mate. I would never tell Jacque that.

LaStacia said that if I give her time, she will let me back in her life and she will eventually be able to tell me everything that is keeping her from doing so right now. I feel encouraged by all of this and I am starting to believe that Senioritis is the best thing that has happened to me up to this point.

Our resident genius, Gemini is looking evil lately. I don't know what the scoop is there, but he seems to be having fun with something. I have never seen him like this before. It is like he is out for revenge or something. That's scary.

This place offers up lots of possibilities.

Alex Green

Life is good. I had a little bout with depression this weekend, but life is still good. When the doctor cuts back on my medication it is hard to keep from feeling anxiety. My anxiety

106

recently is not so much like it was before—not fitting in with anyone socially.

My anxiety is more about Dee Dee. What if it doesn't last. Is there possibly anyone else out there who has something in common with me and that would give me the time of day? Mr. Tompkins would say that there are lots of people out there for me, but that is his job to flower things up.

I was pretty shocked by Dee Dee's reaction when my mom told her that I couldn't go out because I was having an anxiety attack. Dee Dee's response was rare. She didn't. I mean, she didn't respond.

She may just be the girl for me. She just accepted it and everything has been good again this week. It is beyond strange for things to work out so well for me. I'm not complaining. I'll just go with it.

We have spent most of our time in 3-to-5 this week working on the picture plaque for Johnny. Dee Dee designed the plaque and we have ordered it now, but I still have to write the caption. Dee Dee is into poetry and I just like to write in general, so I'm sure we will come up with something special for Johnny in the end.

Everitt and Nakeisha's lyrics seem to be up to Mr. Tompkins standards, so that part of the performance is taken care of. They just need to practice their presentations and their dance moves.

The forensics presentations are almost ready. They had to come up with some presentations that would fit for the event. They seem to have everything in order. They practiced in front of us today and they are pretty good.

Hopefully LaStacia has everything coordinated and choreographed because we are coming up on the day of the presentation and everybody's been hyping this up so much that it better be good.

LaStacia Foster

I felt a little devious telling Lurch about what I had seen with Ricky and Ms. Brown, but I need to keep my actress skills tuned. The musical is next week. The good thing about this thing Gemini and Ricky got me involved in is that it keeps my mind off of Ken and what happened.

I have been doing a lot better and luckily for me, Mr. T wasn't in a preachy mood when I talked to him and he did everything just right. It could have gone either way. I am lucky that I caught him on a good day.

Lurch looked surprised to see me when I walked into his office on Tuesday morning. He asked how I was doing and, of course, he didn't know my name. So, I used my social skills and stuck out my hand, firm grip, and I told him my name and reminded him I run track, and I'm in the musicals and plays.

He feigned remembering, but who knows. Lurch actually thought this was a social visit, so I didn't waste any time getting to the point.

"Mr. Adams, I have stumbled upon something that I really think you need to know about," LaStacia says with a concerned expression on her face.

"Well, what is it LaStacia?" Mr. Adams asks in an authoritative tone.

"It's Ms. Brown."

"Yes, Ms. Brown is one of the very best teachers we have here."

"Yes, I think so too," LaStacia says lowering her tone and silently sobbing.

"LaStacia, what is the problem?"

"The problem is Ms. Brown."

"Yes, you already said that."

"I know, b-b-but Ms. Brown isn't doing what she is supposed to do. She's doing other stuff."

"Like what exactly."

"I can't tell you."

"Okay, well maybe when you feel more up to it you can come back and tell me," Mr. Adams smugly states with a sigh of relief.

"No, now!"

"Okay, now is fine too."

LaStacia spits it all out at once, "Ms. Brown has been having relations with Ricky Terrell in and out of school. I saw them in her room once and at Milford Lake and she is always saying things to him before 3-to-5."

"Well, LaStacia that doesn't mean that Ms. Brown has done something wrong now does it?"

LaStacia uncharacteristically shouts, **"I tried to be nice Mr. Adams. Ms. Brown is having relations with Ricky Terrell. That means she f... him. Do you get it now? Do you?"**

"LaStacia, now I will not have that tone in my office. When you are ready to talk to me in a sane and civil tone, you may come back. Until then, I will not tolerate your tone or your language."

"So, you're not going to do anything about it?" LaStacia yells at Mr. Adams as she walks out of his office with secretaries' jaws dropping as they stare after LaStacia.

"This is not the appropriate way to handle this LaStacia."

"A teacher is having relations with a student and you won't do anything about it until I tell you in a calm tone? Does that mean I have to tell you something you want to hear? You aren't going to do anything about this are you?"

"As far as I am concerned, this conversation never took place. I give no heed to those who do not respect me, my school, or my teachers. Have a nice day, Miss Foster."

As soon as I left the office, the secretaries began talking and, of course there are student aides in there too. So, the high school rumor mill began to churn and once that baby gets started with both adults and students, look out! Everyone in the school will have a theory about what is going on by the end of the day.

Making a scene in front of the secretaries was the best part of the plan. Secretaries have phone access and they use it often. What do you think those ladies are doing while students are answering the incoming calls? They are talking to their network of friends.

That network of friends includes all of the wives of important businessmen in the town, school board members' wives and actual school board members, parents, relatives, et cetera. You name the group and by 2:40 all of them knew something was going on between stud athlete Ricky Terrell and one of the teachers at the school.

Our plan worked to perfection. Nakeisha got herself written up by the terrible two, which established a pattern of peculiar practices. Where did that come from?

Anyway, Nakeisha set up a pattern of behavior that is sure to add to the guilt of Ms. Brown and Mrs. Moore. I think Ms. Brown will be in a little bit more trouble than Mrs. Moore. After all, Mary Kay Letourneau is in jail and Monica Lewinsky is making hand bags and doing exclusive interviews.

The counselor's picked up on the rumor and they are as nosy as they come, so they want the scoop more than they want to help us. Let's be honest, very seldom do counselor's counsel anymore, except with rare counselors on rare occasions. Just ask Mr. T. If counselors were good with kids and actually knew us, then why does Mr. T log so many therapy hours with us?

So, the counselors have been calling us down and the plan was to tell bits and pieces and then act like we couldn't handle talking about it, and slowly let them in on what is going on. Planning for this was easy because there is nothing more predictable than the channels in which high schools go through in a crisis.

The only thing we didn't plan on was Nakeisha's mouth. We should have known better. Nakeisha couldn't keep her mouth shut if she wanted to. We have known her forever and we should have seen this coming. Talk about a predictable occurrence.

Nakeisha was telling everything in and out of the counselor's office. The counselor's told Nakeisha to keep everything strictly confidential, so she told everyone she saw that, "That skanky ho Ms. Brown been sleepin' with Ricky cuz ain't no one her age give her the time o' day and Ricky need to get his grade up."

So now, not only does everyone know that something has been going on, but specifically with who and why. Leave it to Nakeisha to spill it all. Oh well, we eventually wanted the truth to be out, but now this makes it a little trickier with Lurch.

There is no way that he can stand by and let it seem like he is not aware of the fact that a student-teacher affair is going on under his nose and thanks to Nakeisha, right there in front of his face in flashing neon capital letter lights.

Lurch never ceases to amaze me. Every time a community member or school board member brings this up, and I am in listening distance, he acts as though it is the very first time that he has heard these allegations. And, each and every time, he denies that any of this could be happening at his school and definitely not with Ms. Brown.

I bet if it was Mr. T or Mr. Jocular, or that crazy math teacher, Mrs. Delaney they would not even get one second's worth of consideration whether the accusations had evidence or not. Well, that is the way the political arena of public education works. I can see it and I am just a student.

So, Lurch took Nakeisha's mistake and played further into our hands. Lurch is going to eat crow. I don't know if I used that correctly, but my grandpa says something like that when people get what they deserve.

I can't believe that Lurch is going to back Ms. Brown up all the way. That wouldn't be the first time. Gosh, did I say that? I have been around Ricky Terrell and this group way too long.

Because he is willing to go through the fire for Ms. Brown, we have him by his testicles and it seems like we will be able to get everything we wanted from Lurch. I think Gemini knew all along that things would play out like this. He just sits back and smiles that evil little smile that he has acquired over the last month or so.

Now the question is whether or not we will all have the stick-to-itiveness to play this out until the end. I think we will. If I can yell out the "F" word in front of the principal and loud enough for everyone to hear, then I can so ride this out until the end.

Now, where we really have Lurch is that he has heard about abuse or inappropriate relations between a student and a teacher. I am pretty sure that Lurch is required by law to do something about all of this and, although not much time has passed, he has yet to report this to anyone. And, Ms. Brown is still teaching.

I have seen cases like this before and whether a teacher is guilty or not, the norm is for there to be an investigation into the allegation while the teacher takes a short leave of absence with pay. None of this has been reported, so none of the proper steps have been taken and Lurch is going to wish he never messed with 3-to-5 Crew. I think right about now Lurch is experiencing Senioritis.

This distraction has been a good one for me and during this short mass hysteria, I have gotten really close with the very sensitive eye candy, Patrick Mathews. Things are looking better and better.

Nakeisha

I told those fools they don't know me and they don't. I am like Muhammad Ali, I shook up the world! I knew I couldn't of kept my mouth shut if I'd wanted to, so here we are. All these authority figures be drinkin' they Pepto Bismo and shit. They got uncontrollable nerves from the stress I have caused.

I don't care about these people. What have they done for me? How they gonna judge Nakeisha? They don't know me.

I been thinkin' about what we did and the legacy we leavin' behind. There ain't no one that can top this shit. They can try to duplicate it, but that ain't gonna happen, I promise you that.

I make up stuff on people all the time. I make up some good ones too. And, then, they come across me with this? How could I pass up on this rumor? Especially when it ain't even a rumor no way.

Me and lil' freaky Jamaican dude Gemini been talkin' and now that I did somethin' outside the plan, he want me to make sure that I don't tell anyone that Lurch knows about this all and that he learned it from LaStacia and that he ain't tellin' nobody that he knows anything about it. I gave the Gem my word, so he don't have to worry 'bout nothin'.

"Dawg, you know what I heard about Lurch's

sorry ass?" asks Nakeisha with a big shit-eating grin on her face.

"Naw, what's up now?" replies Tayvon, curiously.

"Lurch know the whole time that Ms. Brown be Ricky's personal prostitute and he ain't done shit about it. Not one thing, and LaStacia told him in front of his secretary and the rest of the office secretaries. Can you believe that?"

"Naw, Keisha. I don't believe that. You're making this stuff up again. Why you always playing Nakeisha?"

"Tay-von. Come on, you gotta admit this is too obvious to be made up. You already heard all of the rumors. I'm tellin' ya, this is the real deal."

"Yeah, you're right girl, I already heard all of the rumors. Maybe you are being straight this time."

"Key-sun, get over here. Do you believe what Keisha over here's been telling me?"

You know, I think that Gemini know what he be doin' before he ever do anything. He know me. I think he know me too well. He knew I was gonna go and tell everyone 'bout Lurch and how he ain't said nothin' to nobody about any of this. Gemini knew I couldn'ta kept that kinda stuff secret.

That's dirty. Playin' me like that. It's kinda funny though. Gemini's the only one that can

116

outsmart Keisha like that. He cool. I ain't gonna hold it against him. Some of my tricks got old by now and Gemini kinda fixed my senior year up pretty good. It hasn't been boring.

If it wasn't for Mr. Tompkins, the 3-to-5 Crew and this whole situation, I woulda got bored and done somethin' stupid and got myself kicked outta this joint. I didn't though, and I'm gonna walk across that stage and everyone gonna realize who I am and that I made it.

No one's gonna keep me down ever. I've got some plans for graduation. We'll jus' wait an' see how errything works out.

Gemini

Everything is going according to plan. Lurch has leaped like a little lackey loon, right into my lavish loop of lasciviousness and laughs. Lurch should have never crossed me. His racist dictatorship will see the end of its days, or, at least while I am here, he will be miserable.

I have made copies of the tapes Ricky helped me make and I am going to get the copies all ready to send to various places. We are going to bribe Lurch until we get what we want. If he doesn't comply, then we will still get what we want, but he will pay dearly.

I plan on having Alex go to Lurch and tell him that we have evidence of the misdeeds. We will have Alex say that if he doesn't want to see this in the hands of the local news, the AP wire and all of the school board members, then he better meet our demands and confirm that he has done so by 8:00a the following morning.

Not only will this decide Lurch's fate, but it will also be another much needed confidence boost for Alex. If he can pull this off, he will have conquered a lot of his anxieties. I've already talked to him and he definitely wants to contribute for the Crew.

We will have to rig up another camera on Alex. The only problem is that I can't afford another three hundred dollars for a camera and the equipment. Alex is going to have to use the cell phone like Ricky did. It just isn't characteristic of Alex to carry a cell phone. The school allows us to carry them now, so maybe Lurch won't give it a second thought.

It is imperative that we tape Lurch incriminating himself, so we can make him promise to do a couple of things for us. If Lurch rubs me the wrong way, he will definitely pay in exponential increments more than he will if he just cooperates.

Lurch has put this all on himself and I am pretty sure that the school would not want to waste its valuable educational resources fighting such a clear violation of teacher code. Furthermore, I am absolutely positive that Lurch alone doesn't have near the firepower necessary to fight off what we will bring to the table in an attempt to rightfully defame the character of him and his cohort Ms. Brown on this incredible sinking ship.

Ricky Terrell

I guess I caused quite a stir around here recently, huh? It looks like we have Lurch right where we want him. The only problem I have now is that sleeping with the enemy had kept my head above water in Ms. Brown's class. Well, now I am in danger of failing for sure. I was never really passing anyway.

In addition to that I am failing my weight training class because I informed Coach Renshaw that I didn't need the class and this broke down equipment anymore, since I have full access to K-State facilities. I can't say that Coach didn't warn me because he told me numerous times that if I didn't get it together, I would fail.

I don't have to take weight training over, but I was already supposed to be making English up in 3-to-5 and I haven't been doing it. Mr. T has been on me everyday and everyone keeps telling me how I have so much potential. Everyone has told me how smart I am for so long that I figured that they would pass me if I made a strong effort at the very end.

All I know is that they are not offering English IV in summer school this year, so if I don't pass, I lose my scholarship to K-State because if I don't pass I don't have a diploma and Coach Snyder doesn't play around with that kind of nonsense. I may have really blown it.

I have to admit that I am kind of scared. My whole life has revolved around football and K-State has been looking at me since I was in eighth grade, so I pretty much just expected to end up there. I am not sure that the teachers that just let me slide by because they knew that I could be a professional athlete have done me a great service.

I am so used to teachers coddling me and helping me make it through, that I just expected that it would always be that way. Then, I am in the English class my senior year and I am making it with the teacher, so I figure that I have it made.

I don't regret any of the stuff I did to try and catch Ms. Brown in a deviant act, but I do regret the fact that I didn't listen to her when she said I was failing. No matter where we were or what we were doing, she never compromised her position on the fact that if I didn't turn my work in, I wouldn't be passing. You have to give her credit for that.

I guess I made my own bed, so maybe I ought to start looking at junior colleges. JUCOs will accept me with a GED and maybe I will get better exposure right out of the gate that way. I know that a lot of people will be disappointed. I was going to be a lot of people's "Guy I know in the NFL". Oh, well.

As for Lurch and Gemini's plan. At least I know that I followed through with something in my life. Since K-State's not going to happen, which is extremely disappointing because I was looking forward to seeing Mrs. Moore's game film, I guess I will enjoy watching Lurch and his little clones suffer through this.

I didn't realize that I could be so cruel, but it really isn't that difficult. Especially when the people receiving the cruelty are asses like Lurch.

Patrick Matthews

Ever since this sex scandal occurred, I have been spending a lot more time with LaStacia, and Jacque seems like a bit of an afterthought. I feel bad about saying that my girlfriend is an afterthought, but LaStacia just has so much more personality and depth. I don't know who I am going to see when I watch the musical this weekend.

Honestly, I think that I am going to see LaStacia, but how will this play out with Jacque? We have been dating for a long time, but things kind of started fizzling a while back too. We'll just wait and see.

LaStacia told me most of what happened with her and Ken. She thanked me for my patience and for not giving her advice. I guess that is the last thing she wanted from me. I played my cards right and now I am reaping the rewards of being a "good friend".

I just realized that this girl has meant a lot to me for a very long time. And, the liberating feeling I am experiencing right now is inexplicable. The moment that I decided that I want to be with LaStacia, my entire body felt warm and then I got chills up and down my spine.

Now, every time I think about her, I get the same feeling and I honestly do not feel bad about dumping Jacque. I will always be friends with Jacque, but we are just that, friends. The hard part will be breaking it to Jacque. I guess I'll just wait and see.

"Jacque, we need to talk."

"What's up, Pat?"

"I think we need to stop seeing each other. I just don't feel like the connection is there any more."

"You know, Pat, we've been together for a while now and I felt horrible because I've been feeling exactly the same way. I think we just kept going out because it was easy, but I haven't felt the attraction we had before for about a couple of months now."

"Really? Me too Jacque, and I was scared to let you know how I was feeling, especially right before the musical and I thought you would be pretty upset that I decided to go for LaStacia and..."

"What? Wait a minute, I thought you were breaking up with me, but LaStacia? How could you? And right before the musical. **You Jerk!**" Jacque screams at the top of her lungs as she pounds Patrick on his chest and runs out.

"Jacque, wait, we aren't going out or anything, I just. Jacque! **Hey! Wait up!**"

Jacque stands by the wall with her head down sobbing and gasping for air. Patrick gently puts his hand on her shoulder and tries to console her.

"Jacque, I am so sorry. I didn't mean to make you cry. I just felt so comfortable and like we were close friends still, so I decided to tell you everything that was on my mind and..."

"Gotcha! Ha ha, I really had you going, didn't I?"

"Hey, that's not even cool."

"That's why they call us drama queens. I bet Stacia couldn't have even pulled that off."

"Well, I'm glad you are not really mad at me, and you know that I will always be your friend."

"I know. I love you Patrick."

"I love you too, Jacque."

Breaking up with Jacque was the most bittersweet thing I have ever done. I will never regret breaking it off with her, but I will never have another first experience of major committed dating again. We learned together, we grew together, and strangely, we grew apart together too.

Enough of this seriousness. I so need to talk to Stacia.

Alex Green

I am not so sure about following through with The Crew's plans. It just doesn't feel right, but for some reason it is not making me overly anxious. Maybe I should do it.

They want me to catch Lurch incriminating himself. Lurch is a jerk, I have to admit. Something about this feels wrong to me, though. I guess it is just that I have never paid enough attention to anyone to be able to get them like we are getting Lurch.

I try to stay invisible as much as possible. That is the way people have always wanted me to be, so I have routinely stayed out of everybody's way. Maybe this is my chance to break those walls down. I have gained a lot of confidence, and my therapist says that confidence will cut back on my anxiety attacks that leave me bedridden.

I am going to do it. Dee Dee seems to think that The Crew has to stick together and she is the only good thing that has ever happened to me. I don't want to let her down.

LaStacia Foster

I am still feeling the aftermath of my little

scene in and out of Mr. Adams' office. I am the ultimate drama queen. Like I mentioned, it was a good distraction for me too. In fact, it was real good. Before our Saturday night performance, one of the stage crew handed me a dozen roses and a card from Patrick Matthews.

It said that he wants to take me out for a celebratory dinner after the last performance and have our first of many dates. A little presumptuous, (Gemini is really rubbing off) but he is quite the handsome man. I can't wait.

I have never made real good choices with men. Maybe this time will be different. I am stronger now and if Patrick messes up, I know I can break it off. I have a feeling that I won't have to worry about things like that right now.

I guess The Crew got to Alex. He decided to participate in our little spy missions now too. On Saturday night Alex sat behind Lurch at the musical. He tapped him on the shoulder and asked if all of the things that I said to him in the office had been looked into and resolved.

Lurch was caught a little bit off guard, so he responded by saying, "How did you know that I had a conversation with Miss Foster about Ms. Brown and Ricky's affair?"

"That's just what I heard, Mr. Adams," replied Alex with a whole lot of extra confidence.

"There is no truth to it son, let it go. Ms. Brown would never do such a thing."

"Thank you for your time, sir."

Mr. Adams is too sure of himself sometimes. Now we have him on tape admitting that he has withheld evidence of maltreatment of a student by a teacher. He admitted that I had reported this to him prior. We have him now, the jerk.

I can't wait to see his face when Gemini presents him with the evidence, our plan of action, and his options of reaction. This ought to be good. The rest of our year should go exactly the way Gemini planned it.

Senioritis isn't bad for us, but it sure is putting a damper on everyone else's year. I guess that is why the faculty and staff don't really like seniors much.

They were afraid of what the world had to offer when they were seniors too. But, at the same time, they are jealous that we have our whole lives ahead of us, we are fiesty and rebellious like they were many moons ago, and we just might do more with our lives than they did.

It makes sense to be jealous of our youth because they (the adults) can never recapture theirs.

The date with Patrick was nice. It was a little awkward, but still nice. Patrick had no expectations of anything physical and he was the perfect gentleman. If he is patient, things will go really well. I just need time to discover the new stronger me. I like what I am seeing already.

I started by walking away from Ken. The next

step was to stand up to an adult ass, Mr. Adams. I did that. I made him make a scene and deny the occurrence of our conversation. Now, I have to prove to myself that I can have a man in my life and still have my life.

What I mean is that I have to be in control of me. No man can ever have that privilege again. I can be someone's partner, but none of this Promise Keepers, man as head-of-the-household and women stay home, listen to your man and don't ever show intelligence stuff. I have to be me, not some man's perception of what I should be.

I am too smart, too proud and too important to this world to be stifled by some man and his ideas of how my world should create his paradise. Not gonna do it.

Gemini

Everything is going according to plan. LaStacia performed like a star. Alex confidently stepped up to the plate and acquired the necessary admittance of guilt. Now it is my turn to turn up the heat a little bit.

I am going to enjoy this. I have been thinking about revenge since I was wrongfully sentenced by the racist, pompous, fearless leader of our high school. I don't truly think he took us seriously as human beings. The irony is that in our group affectionately known as Senioritis or The Crew, we have the school's most intelligent kids.

Lurch looks upon us as a loud-mouthed riot machine, a genius child of questionable genetics, an NFL prospect whose use in this school has passed, a plagiarist with annoying "important" parents, a manic-depressive outsider, a pot head with thuggish tendencies, his friend the pot head, and a second-rate actress who embarrassed him to get in this group and she is an embarrassment to herself with her lackluster attempt to make Lurch look like an ass.

Lurch is wrong about us and he has been wrong about just about every kid who has walked through the school doors. Nakeisha is right. He don't know us. He doesn't. A lot of his favorite teachers are like that too.

People like Lurch are the outsiders. They always have been. They are people who have always had to do something to prove who they are. If Lurch would give respect he would get respect.

I bet when he was in high school, he spent most of his time putting people down to raise himself up. That works in high school. Well, it at least keeps you from the bottom rung. The only problem is that becomes habit and it works less in college.

Then, the way I see it, you grow up to have a job where you can tell people what to do to satisfy yourself. That makes people like Lurch feel BIG. It starts with dominating kids and having all order all the time, which teaches kids to fear and not learn anything.

The people who become educators and don't like kids have issues and baggage. You can't be an educator and not like kids. You can't unless you don't like yourself. I don't think Lurch likes himself. He is proud of himself, cocky and unbearable. But, when he looks in the mirror, I don't think he likes what he sees.

A lot of kids and a lot of adults are right there with Lurch. They are confident on the outside, but they don't like who they are. The problem with guys like Lurch is that he takes that feeling that he gets when he looks in the mirror, and he makes everyone who he judges as unworthy human beings feel as bad as that image in the mirror feels.

Unfortunately, too many teachers follow guys like Lurch, they don't get to know who the students are, and consequently, a lot of kids from a lot of shitty backgrounds find the same road blocks at school that they find at home. When everywhere a young person turns there is a road block, they begin feeling like they are worthless and that they can't do anything to make anyone notice them as valuable humans.

Sadly, that is what people like Lurch want to happen. They feed off of being right about kids who they say won't make it. When, all the while they should be doing everything in their power to make sure those kids find their way and prove the world wrong.

Guys like Mr. T know that and he is no genius. He just takes the time to know kids, listen to what they have to say, and he shows them that there is at least one person in the world that believes in them and will cheer for them on their journey to success.

Now, I usually don't go off on rants like that. Especially not in words that people understand. But, if I have learned anything from Senioritis, it is that condescending doesn't make me better than others, it makes me out of touch with reality, cocky, inconsiderate, presumptuous and, worst of all, just like Lurch.

"Mr. Adams, I have a proposition for you," Gemini says as he catches Mr. Adams doing hall duty after school.

"Gemini, now is not the time or the place for this discussion," replies Mr. Adams with a stern, unforgiving look of disgust on his face.

Gemini lets Mr. Adams listen to the tape of himself telling Alex that he has previously spoken to LaStacia about Ms. Brown's affair. Mr. Adams looks stupefied, turns pale and tells Gemini they need to talk right away in his office. The Crew looks on with indescribable joy.

Patrick Matthews

Good news, I am salutatorian again thanks to Gemini. I guess his little talk with Lurch got us what we all wanted. Gemini was going to be valedictorian no matter what, but his ultimate goal was somewhat larger.

The conversation between Lurch and Gemini produced lots of results. Gemini is valedictorian of our class, which wasn't really an issue. But, I am once again salutatorian, which puts me back where I belong. I thought it didn't mean a lot, and in the larger scheme of things, it really doesn't matter.

It just feels good to get some sort of vindication. I don't mean toward Miss Becker, but against Lurch. I already made my piece with the Miss Becker situation. I was wrong. Enough said.

However, that being said, Gemini guaranteed that my and Stacia's records will be cleared as of today. There will be no hint of our issues on record anywhere. Gemini made Lurch show him our files to prove that there were no marks on our records. Gemini is a tough man to negotiate with.

Gemini also used his bribe evidence to get a few more things. Gemini truly is the smartest person I know. Even Mr. Tompkins can't hold a candle to the raw mental ability of the Gem.

Gemini also got Jamal an honorary degree.

They took Jamal off of life support yesterday and things aren't looking too good.

None of us knows how to react to this. I guess we have been trying to get our minds off of Jamal by remembering him through the work of The Crew.

Jamal's mom is going to accept the honorary degree. She is very proud to receive the degree and she is going to be able to say a few words in Jamal's honor. Jamal just couldn't quit his habits in time. We are going to miss him. We have missed him, but really, he has been with us every step of the way.

Gemini is to be the last speaker before the diplomas are handed out. I think Gemini enjoys the opportunity to have the last word.

After graduation is over, Gemini has set it up so that he can go to the Manhattan Town Center Mall and present the picture plaque and set the dedication date for the benches that will be placed in various locations throughout the mall in honor of Johnny. Jumar will be accepting the picture plaque alongside of Johnny. This will be a huge moment for both of them.

Gemini says that he also opened the possibility of having a guest speaker this year at graduation. He wouldn't even tell me who it is going to be, so I guess we will all wait and see. In recent years we have not had any guest speakers because the best we can get consists of state representatives and the governor of Kansas. Those people are boring and none of us wants to hear their message. They don't live in, or come from the same world that we do.

I am excited to see who the guest speaker is going to be. If I know Gemini, it ought to be interesting and someone who will not only make the crowd roar, but also make the administration crawl. This ought to be fun.

Gemini also set it up so that we can have just one letter to the administration from our group. We all gave our input, and Gemini agreed to place a combination of what we wanted to have said and his own thoughts about our year, our future, and our experience with senioritis in his graduation speech, which will serve as our letter.

Unfortunately for Ricky, Gemini was not able to pull any strings to help him graduate. He is going to have to live with his lack of effort. He seems to be handling it well. I don't know if I could.

He has been talking about getting his GED and going to JUCO, but that usually ends up being a wash because JUCOs are usually in towns that are way too far from home and with a lot less notoriety than a football powerhouse like K-State. I hope he sticks it out. He truly is the most talented athlete this school has seen in a long time.

When Gemini first told me of the progress he had made, I have to admit I was skeptical. Lurch is no dummy. He is not just going to let someone march into his office and make demands. But,

Gemini got all of the negotiated agreements read, witnessed, and notarized, so I guess Mr. Adams has no choice but to follow through with all of his promises.

Gemini says that whether he agreed to the demands or not, he is still going to have to pay for allowing Ms. Brown to do what she did without any disciplinary actions.

This year's graduation ought to be one of epic proportions. No one will ever forget graduation day and the day senioritis won out over the haters out there in educational la la land.

Gemini—The Graduation Speech

Friends, family, classmates, welcome to the class of 2004 graduation. I have thought long and hard about what I wanted to say on this very moment and I have to tell you it is not easy, even for me, to come up with the right words. I have written several speeches, but none of them are what you guys want to hear. So, I have decided to speak from the heart and try to express the sentiments of my classmates.

I have been lucky enough to spend most of this semester with a group of peers who ended up finding themselves confined to Mr. Tompkins classroom for the 3-to-5 Program. I know that if I would have turned in a speech that acknowledges this program or its worth to the school, it would not have been approved. Our group is also affectionately known as Senioritis.

All of you have heard this term before and you all know what you think it means. Senioritis is a disease all seniors acquire either the first part, last part, or the whole part of their senior year. Senioritis is a term made up by teachers to describe the apathetic attitudes of most members of the senior class during their senior year. Most look at the seniors as unmotivated, selfish, and too arrogant for their own good.

Those people are **WRONG**.

I want to tell you a story about Senioritis. It includes individual students from our senior class, but it also includes a little bit of all of you to some extent. My story is about a group of mismatched misfits who all fell victim to different circumstances with the same result. We all ended up in the 3-to-5 Program because of an unethical person and some bad decisions on our part.

This person made quick judgements on the lives of a genius child of questionable genetics, a loud-mouthed riot machine, an NFL prospect whose use to this school has passed, a plagiarist with annoying "important" parents, a manic-depressive outsider, a pot head with thuggish tendencies, his friend the pot head comedian rapper, and a second-rate actress. These are not my perceptions, but they are definitely his. He looks at all of you as one of his cookie cutter descriptions.

He wasn't prepared for Senioritis.

We aren't stereotypical cookie cutter carbon copies of any description concocted in the head of this man. We are individuals with emotions and feelings; we react to situations, we grow, we learn, and the part that really surprised this man is that we are way too intelligent for our own good. We don't just lie down and take unwarranted punishments; we defend ourselves and try to find ways to right our wrongs.

Where this nameless man went wrong with us and with most of our graduating class is he expected respect without ever giving us an inkling of it. We are worth more than that. All of us are. We deserve better.

I am here to tell you today that we will have better. I am here to tell you that we can right the wrongs, fight the power, and create an ethical environment for the future graduating classes. Mr. Tompkins told us when we were freshmen that we were responsible for changing our school.

Well, now is not too late for that, nor is it too late to change our futures. We are not moving to the real world from here. That is all a lie. This is the real world. If we can't get along with our peers and stand up for ourselves now, we will have a hard time making it from here on out.

I am here to challenge you to stand up for yourselves. Be sure of who you are. Make a change in your life. Don't let others tell you that you can't make it. That was their life, not yours.

Although most of you look at me as geeky smart, I hadn't stood up for myself very much in my life. I haven't had to. I am here to tell you today that Senioritis has spread and the administration is petrified by it.

I want you, the class of 2004, to leave here today knowing that we can make waves. When you leave today with your diplomas, go straight home, shower, change your clothes, and while you are getting ready to go to Project Graduation for our last formal time together as a group, turn on your televisions and catch the news.

This world is changing. This school is changing. We are all changing. We are the catalysts for the change. When you turn on your televisions tonight and watch the evening news, you will see the changes first hand. You will no longer believe that you can't make a difference.

The rest of our lives people will be telling us that we will not make it. That should be our motivation to succeed. After tonight, you, the class of 2004, will see that our legacy is change, revolution, liberation, and never again will you have to worry about our future generations being kept down by any power hungry individuals.

He was wrong about you. He was wrong about us. When he thought he had us beaten he was really wrong. I think by now you all have an idea who he is. When his bell rings tonight right before the evening news, and he answers the door, "You rang?" all of the wrongs he supposedly sought out and obliterated will turn into a list of rights that he may not expect.

So, class of 2004, be strong, know who you are, fight for yourselves, never let anyone try to keep you down. Prove to the world that Senioritis is more than a disorder. Prove that Senioritis is just a push to our next phase of life. It is something for doubters to feel when we leave, and for us to use as motivation to never look back, always look forward, and never let anyone put us down without a fight. Thank You.

Alex Green Looking Back—
10 years later...

The graduation speech went great. Everyone stood up for Gemini and gave him a standing ovation. Gemini ended graduation making everyone wonder what the big sweeping change would be on the evening news. After Gemini spoke, each student came up to receive their diploma.

Traditionally, the valedictorian receives their diploma last. As soon as Gemini received his diploma, he took out his cell phone and dialed three different phone numbers. Each time someone answered on the other end he would say, "Go with it, I am in the clear. Run the story."

Before Gemini ever spoke, Jamal's mom spoke

138

just as Gemini had planned. Mrs. Lee accepted the time allotted to her, but she did not accept the honorary degree. She surprised everyone. She spoke very eloquently as we all sat in awe hanging on to every word she had to say.

"To the class of 2004, I would like to say thank you for the honor meant to be bestowed on my son, Jamal Lee. Jamal passed away this morning after living a short time after we took him off of life support. I love Jamal and I know a lot of you love him too.

I decided to not accept a diploma for Jamal after reading through his journal from the 3-to-5 program. In his journal, he wrote about the conversations he had with Mr. T and how he knew that Mr. T was right, and that he should stop smoking weed and get back to the smart kid with good grades that he always was.

I decided not to accept the honorary diploma for Jamal because, although I love him, he does not deserve to be honored for something he did not complete. That sends the absolute wrong message to you, his peers.

I want you kids to understand that Jamal died because he had to get high one more time. Don't think this is a 'Just Say No' speech; it is not. Using any kind of drug or alcohol can be dangerous. Jamal ended his life because he got high, because he got high, because he got high.

Cute lyrics right? Funny song, right? Well,

it's funny until the universe catches you. Those are words Jamal wrote, words he learned in Mr. Tompkins English I class, words that he learned from a short story about a kid who got caught by the universe and it ruined him.

Jamal is dead because he thought he was invincible and that Mr. Tompkins was just being preachy. Jamal is dead because a drug that you all say is not addictive, left him wanting one more high time. We can't bring Jamal back and he hasn't earned a diploma, what I want you to take from Jamal's death is some advice:

Do not ever think you are bigger than anything that can alter your mind or perceptions. Jamal thought he was bigger. He thought he had all of time. Now, his time is up and he didn't even begin to live. You are all just beginning your lives. If the rest of your lives are focused on the next time you get to go out and get high or drunk one more time, remember Jamal and ask yourself what is more important, getting high or living? Thank you very much."

We knew Jamal's mom was going to touch us, but we didn't know that Jamal had passed. I think Jamal made a bigger impact on our class than anyone would have ever imagined by dying on the day of graduation. The shock of the death made Mrs. Lee's words more effective than she could have ever planned.

Even more surprising was the guest speaker. Gemini chose Mr. Adams. Can you believe that? Of all people, Gemini chooses the one who we hate the most. I guess it was a test. Mr. Adams' last chance to do right.

"I am extremely honored to be chosen as the guest speaker for the class of 2004. As you all know, you are a very special group of young people. We have had minimal problems this year and no major issues have come up. I have to say that the success of this class is due in large part to the fine faculty here at our school.

This year more than any other, I have seen the faculty working closely with the students, and creating a better learning environment with individual attention. I think our faculty deserves a round of applause.

Also, none of you could have ever made it here if it weren't for the love and support of your parents. I feel so very lucky to have been given the opportunity to speak to you today and I will keep this very brief.

I want you to leave this place remembering three very important rules to live by:

    1. Always be honest. Honesty will get you everywhere;

    2. Don't be afraid to look for help, there are always going to be people willing to give it to you;

    3. Trust your mentors and peers to

always do the right thing and they will
never let you down.

If you follow those simple rules, life will treat
you kindly and you will make it in this world.
Thank you."

I have never heard a more hypocritical speech
in my life, but that is only because I know what
this leads up to. Before graduation, when Gemini
set up some rules in his bargain with Lurch,
Gemini wrote some other stipulations in the fine
print.

Gemini originally had personally and through
third party threats, guaranteed that if demands
weren't met, he would have evidence sent to the
associated press, local news, et cetera. I guess the
threats were not idle. The funny part is Gemini
planned on sending the evidence, no matter wh
Lurch agreed or didn't agree on, if Mr. Ada
was not genuine in his speech to the class.

Gemini is Dr. Evil. Lurch obviously did not
give a genuine speech, so Gemini sent out the
evidence the day of graduation as soon as he had
his degree in hand.

There was an uproar in the Junction City,
Kansas community the day after graduation.
Gemini really shook things up with his devilish
deviousness.

As soon as students, parents, and community
members alike got home and watched the evening
news, all of the coded "he's" and "this person's" in

142

Gemini's graduation speech suddenly made sense. Especially the part about when he answers the door, "You rang," and about "obliterating wrongs," and "getting rights he didn't expect," we should have understood then.

Gemini was talking about Lurch answering his door when the police showed up to question him in the sexual harassment case that he covered up. The unexpected rights Gemini mentioned were Miranda rights.

Mr. Adams is required by law to report sexual harassment or misconduct to the authorities when he learns of any such thing. This is especially true when the charges are on a teacher harassing a student. Mr. Adams is guilty of negligence and a recent court case awarded a single victim over 100 million dollars for negligence of an administrator in reporting the harassment of a student by a teacher.

Ricky Terrell and Diana Brown could have been considered consenting adults; however, Ricky is a minor and a student, and he was seduced by Ms. Brown in her own classroom. That is one issue. The other issue is that Mr. Adams knowingly ignored the report of sexual misconduct of a student and a teacher, even after hearing direct evidence of the occurrence.

Gemini already knew all about every bit of this legal stuff before he ever put his plan together. I guess he had read about some sort of civil rights statutes. And, he also knew of something called

Title IX. Needless to say, both Mr. Adams and Ms. Brown were in for a rude awakening. The school district may also have some liability issues since Mr. Adams was knowingly indifferent to the sexual misconduct.

Gemini told me, "Schools are strictly liable for sexual misconduct when those schools have actual knowledge of the misconduct and still fail to adequately respond. Especially if the person with the knowledge has the authority to adequately respond but is 'knowingly indifferent'."

That pretty much says Ms. Brown and Lurch are screwed. And, the school district better try to make a settlement outside of court before they're into the millions of dollars range. If Lurch would have done his job properly, the district would have no worries. Lucky for us Lurch is as dumb as he looks. He was completely knowingly indifferent. That pretty much sums up his existence in our school.

If Ricky seeks restorative justice, he has a pretty good case. How could he lose if Gemini is in his corner? Gemini could probably be his lawyer. The irony of Gemini's speech did not escape anyone when they heard all of the news.

I have to admit, Gemini made a very interesting end to our year. There was no shortage of information to talk about at Project Graduation. I think it was the first time on record that no one left early. Everyone wanted the scoop on what had been going on and how long did we know all of this was going to happen.

Nobody believed any of us when we told them that none of The Crew knew where Gemini was going to take all of this information. We thought he was just going to bribe Mr. Adams and leave it at that. We all got what we wanted after all.

I guess, in the end, Ricky got what he wanted too. The reason to strive to be a pro athlete is money. Well, on the news we heard that Ricky had already filed suit and the school had no comment on the issue. Gemini couldn't help Ricky graduate, but he may have gotten him rich nonetheless.

As you can imagine, all of our peers were wanting one thing more than anything else. They all wanted to see the tapes, the perverts. Half the night was spent by most of the male population of our senior class trying to create their own fantasy of how the details of Ricky and Ms. Brown's affair played out. They came up with the wildest stuff.

Actually, they weren't too far off on a lot of their assumptions. Truth is truly stranger than fiction. There is no doubt about that in my mind.

Early in the night Gemini got all of The Crew together to discuss what we could and could not talk about tonight. We did our best to not ruin Ricky's case. It was difficult though.

Lurch was so wrong to cross Gemini. If he only would have known in the beginning that Gemini was going to make the disciplinary action taken toward him so personal, maybe Lurch would have reconsidered. No, Lurch has always been way too sure of himself to admit that a student may be able to outsmart him.

Gemini kept reminding us that it was a group effort. But, we didn't buy it for a second. We are all relatively smart, but Gemini knew what he was doing from the very beginning. He had everything planned out. We were all just pawns in his chess match.

He was a puppeteer pulling strings and watching his subjects follow through with each movement expertly. Gemini made our high school experience one that we would never forget.

Immediately after the news reports, the school district quickly investigated the charges and quickly dismissed Mr. Adams and Ms. Brown by the next afternoon. If the district wouldn't have acted swiftly, the community would have been calling for resignations of everyone from the superintendent down.

You can't fault the district, though. The district had no knowledge of the affair. Mr. Adams never reported even a part of what had occurred. The district was really caught off guard.

Unfortunately, Mr. Adams had no trouble finding a new job. A nearby district in Manhattan, Kansas picked Mr. Adams up as head principal immediately following their own uproar. There had been a push in the community to rid the school of the Indian mascot. The motion was quickly voted down.

The person who made the push for the mascot makeover was the current principal of Manhattan's high school. That principal was fired immediately at the end of the year. Mr. Adams will fit right in at this school. He is coming in on the heels of a principal being fired for trying to remove a racist symbol that was somehow supposedly representative of a mostly white school population. Lurch couldn't have found a better home.

Ms. Brown decided to go back to school at K-State so she can teach college students and still hang out with the former Mrs. Moore. For some reason, Mrs. Moore's relationship with her husband was in shambles by the end of the year. Go figure. I'm sure the divorce had everything to do with Mr. Moore and nothing to do with K-State's star quarterback.

Ricky never did get access to that "game film". Trust me, we asked him repeatedly. Mrs. Moore is unethical, not ugly.

Ms. Brown will have a whole pool of eligible college students to choose from and she could probably thank the Manhattan Mercury for all of the publicity it gave her. Who needs a personal ad when you are front page news?

Fortunately for the upcoming classes at Junction City High School, Mr. Jocular is now the principal of the school. I don't think there could be a more deserving man than Mr. Nicholas Jocular, boyhood pal of Tommy Tompkins.

I would say Mr. Tompkins would be an even better choice, but taking him out of the classroom to discipline full time, make policy and be a political figurehead just doesn't fit his laid-back personality. Students need Mr. Tompkins to get them started off on the right foot as freshmen and to be there to guide them for as long as they might possibly need him after that.

The whole structure of the school changed after our senior year. The 3-to-5 Program no longer exists because there are several other options for both discipline, and course credit availability. I am kind of happy that the program was ended after our senior year. That makes The Crew a legacy and Senioritis a copyrighted feeling that was invented by generations before us, but redefined by a small group of misguided misfits who shook up the whole institution of learning known as high school.

Aside from the school business, the presentation of the picture plaque in honor of Johnny went great. Gemini made a nice speech and Jumar said a few words about Johnny being his hero. There wasn't a dry eye in the mall. The plaque is at the entrance of Town Center Mall, and there are benches in various location in the mall that have small golden signs on them which read, "Reserved for Johnny and all the friends of his choice—Dedicated by his favorite brother,

Jumar." Everyone who knows Johnny befriends him, so the small, engraved signs are just a reminder to people to acknowledge Johnny, and be a friend to him.

Johnny was also presented with a gift certificate for free unlimited refills of his two-liter at any restaurant in the Food Court. Each bench has a cup holder big enough for a two-liter to fit into, and there is a small storage area behind each bench for Johnny, or mall patrons to place their bags while they relax, or eat, or whatever.

Jumar was so proud of his brother. Johnny was so happy that he danced, and ran through the mall most of the rest of the day, sitting on his benches and asking for his free refills. Johnny finally feels like his life has purpose and Jumar can now rest easy knowing that Johnny will never be alone or feel insignificant again.

You may be wondering why the last heading says **Alex Green—10 years after graduation.** Well, I decided to write a book about our experience in the 3-to-5 program after spending the last ten years as a journalist for the Topeka Capitol Journal. Mr. Tompkins encouraged me to be a writer and I finally have enough confidence to write down all of our experiences from 2004.

In order to write this book, I figured I would need the voices of my fellow 3-to-5 Crew. The only problem would be getting down how they felt 10 years ago. Then, it hit me. We wrote journals our entire time in Mr. Tompkins program. If he kept our journals, my book could come from that.

I called Mr. Tompkins about 6 months ago and asked him if he still had the journals. He told me that it was good to hear from me and that he was impressed with some of my editorials. Then, in pure Mr. Tompkins form, he said I could have the journals if I got permission from each of my former classmates. The big catch was me getting all of The Crew together for a reunion in Mr. Tompkins room in order to let each other know what we mean to each other, and to make sure that we all really wanted the information in our journals to come out.

Mr. Tompkins is the same guy he has always been. He made sure we would have to be reunited, have a reason to talk to each other, and he made sure that we would all come back and see him. Mr. Tompkins told us a long time ago that once we left, we would come back maybe once in the first year and then we wouldn't come anywhere close to the high school. Once again, he was right.

So, I called up The Crew and each member agreed to show up on the 4th of July, 2014. I have never looked forward to anything more in my life. Each phone call was a complete treat. After reminiscing for a short time with each of my classmates, I gave each one of them an assignment that Mr. Tompkins thought would be a good idea for them to do.

I told each of my friends that they needed to create one last journal entry to tell what they are doing now and anything else they may want to add. Whatever they want. Mr. Tompkins said I should promise to put the journals in my book.

We had a great time with our reunion. No one had really changed all that much. I guess I am the only one who has made a major transformation. After we talked, went out, hung out, and then left and went our separate ways, everyone agreed to allow me to use their journal entries. Nakeisha reminded me to not forget her if I make it big. Mr. Tompkins reminded me not to misrepresent him and to make him look smart. Everyone else just wanted to see the finished product.

Since I am now finished with compiling the old journals and situations into a book, I want to finish this off in the style I began. Each of us will speak in turn, but I have to switch the order. It wouldn't be right without Nakeisha getting the last word.

Gemini

When Alex contacted me, I was ecstatic. I hadn't heard from any of The Crew except Everitt since the summer of our senior year. I owe a lot of my success to that group of people at that time in my life.

I had always thought that I would have to be a nuclear physicist since everyone looked at me as a genius. The Crew helped me realize that there are many forms of genius. I look at each member of The Crew as their own sort of genius.

Alex wanted an update on what has happened to The Crew over the last ten years. I was on the path to become a medical doctor when I realized that was not my passion. Mr. Tompkins told us that the most important thing is not what job you have or how much monetary gain your job will help you acquire, but the important thing is that you select a job that you love doing and you don't dread showing up for.

I thought about this long and hard. I came up with my decision and I have never looked back. I am a video game designer for my own company known as Gemini Games. I love going to work, I get to play with the finished products, and I am filthy rich.

I have had to learn how to speak in plain language. I write the instruction booklets for my games and I remember when I was just a mere game player, how hard the instruction booklets were to understand. Especially the manuals for role-playing games. Right before Alex contacted me I got a phone call from my biggest client ever. I am going to be making a game to coincide with the latest Harry Potter film. My game will go up for sale as soon as the seventh installment in the series comes out this Christmas.

I learned a lot from Mr. Tompkins and The Crew. The most valuable lesson I learned is to never let anyone tell you that something is not possible. I am very intelligent, but I don't have to be a doctor or a lawyer or a nuclear physicist to prove it. I am as smart as I ever was and I am a video game designer.

Ricky Terrell

I couldn't believe my ears when I heard Alex's voice on the phone. He has really done well for himself. My senior year was my wake-up call. I realized after my senior year that I had been coddled way too long, and I was going to have to learn to live without everyone holding my hand all the time.

It was really hard. I tried to go to JUCO, but I missed my mom and home so much that I quit after my first season. I never went back to school and I had to find a job here in Junction City.

I have been working at Jim Clark's, a local auto dealership and I have been doing pretty well for myself. The first few years I made a lot of sales just from name recognition. I guess you have to use your resources. It has worked out pretty good so far.

I am one of the top car salesmen in the city and I provide for my family. I am married and have two little girls. My wife already had the children before we got married. I am a sucker for older women—No big surprise.

Oh yeah, I won the lawsuit over the district. I had to put the money in a trust fund that could only be used for the advancement of children through education or mentoring.

Patrick Matthews

Wow! It was such a shock to hear from Alex. I am excited to see what he is able to piece together for his book. My senior year shaped my life. I am who I am today because of that year.

I could have done a lot of things after graduating from Junction City High School. I had great grades, lots of friends, and I had a full-ride scholarship for college. I decided to do what would make me the happiest. I became a teacher.

I actually student taught for Mr. Tompkins before I began teaching. I became a teacher because I realized that I respected the effect I could have on so many kids. Plus, I respect the amount of patience it takes to be a teacher.

After helping LaStacia out in high school, I had considered becoming a therapist, but I wanted an occupation where I would be able to get new clients every four years. That way, I could watch my clients grow and move on with their lives without having to know any more than they are willing to tell. I wanted to reach kids without having to see all the shitty stuff up front.

The last six years have been great. I am a high

154

school English teacher at Topeka Highland Park in Topeka, Kansas. The school has a similar racial diversity to Junction City, and I feel like I am making a difference.

The first few years I contacted Mr. Tompkins a lot. There were situations I wasn't ready for. I ran into several situations where I had to make the decision to either turn in a student's parents for abuse, or leave the situation alone and watch the child fight through the problems until they could get out of their houses at age eighteen.

I have chosen to not report situations many times because I made the mistake of reporting a child's parents after the student had told me bad personal things that had happened to him. This abuse had been occurring for most of his life, so I should have known better than to report it. All I ended up doing was making his life more miserable and more unmanageable than before.

It has been a learning experience, but it has also been as great as Mr. Tompkins told me it would be. He told me before I took this job that if I was not going to form relationships with my students, if I was not going to learn insurmountable patience, or if I was going to constantly complain about how little I make, that I should consider doing something else.

I made the right choice and I have no regrets. I am working on my masters in administration, so I may return to Junction City, Kansas to become the greatest administrator the school has ever seen.   Mr. Jocular may have something to say about that, but I look forward to returning some day.

Alex Green

Well, I have to put my name in the mix just like all of my former classmates. I had a tough time right after we graduated. I went through another bout with depression. It turns out that Dee Dee was too good to be true.

We did have a lot in common, but Ricky made her go out with me. She broke up with me the day after graduation. I am not too mad at Ricky. He was just trying to help me out and boost my self-esteem.

I should have known better. Guys like me don't ease into situations like that very often, if ever. I thank God for unanswered prayers, though. If I would have ended up with Dee Dee, I would have never met my wife, or acquired my job at the Topeka Capitol Journal.

When I called up The Crew, I also called up Dee Dee and told her I would like to meet her for lunch. During high school, I was the outsider who no one paid attention to, and she was my girlfriend out of sympathy. I felt a lot better after I talked to her.

She admits that she made a mistake. She went out with me because Ricky guilted her into it, but she says she didn't know what she had until she broke up with me. She says she has had an empty feeling ever since. She hasn't had any luck with men. They have treated her pretty rotten.

. She said she can't stay in a relationship now because she always has the feeling that something is missing. She also said she hasn't felt a connection with anyone like she felt with me and that makes it hard for any man to live up to.

That did a lot for my self-esteem. The woman I married didn't know much about how other people viewed me in high school. Her only knowledge of me was from the journalism classes we shared and she thought I was witty. Who would have thunk it? I hope everyone will like how I piece together our past in my novel.

Everitt Jackson

I was really happy to hear from Alex and I look forward to seeing The Crew. Wow, I can't believe it has been ten years. My life has sure changed. I went from being the kid that needed help, to the man that finds the solutions for kids' problems.

After Jamal died, I thought long and hard about how I could make a difference. I knew that I wanted to help kids make sure they didn't make the same mistakes Jamal and I made. I talked a lot to Mr. Tompkins about what I could do to make things better for kids and he said I should contact Ricky T and build a teen center.

I thought he was nuts, but then he explained what he had in mind. It wasn't going to be like the teen centers that everyone always talks about building that lose support and everyone says they knew it wouldn't make it.

Mr. T described a place where the kids could play sports, video games, and have dances with radio DJs scheduled regularly. Mr. T said as long as there was consistency and if the center could actually have things that kids wanted to do, that it would work great.

So, I run a teen center funded by Ricky T's trust fund. I guess the teen center falls under advancement of children or mentoring.

At the center, kids can pay to play video games in groups by the hour. We have three big screen televisions just for video games. Gemini donated the televisions and the game systems.

We have a dance floor and we have dances every Friday and Saturday night for high school kids and we have dances every Tuesday night for middle schoolers. We have two basketball courts that can convert into volleyball courts. We have two movie theater rooms with projectors donated by the local theater when they went to digital. We can still get the older style films, so we have a movie night once a week. During that day we show little kid movies and have several matinees. We also have a room where kids can pick out their own DVDs and watch them per our approval.

We also have a professional therapist that comes in once a week. And, during the week we had two counselors that were there on a rotating basis. When those two go on vacation, Mr. Tompkins substitutes.

I think Jamal would be proud. My center is named **THE JAMAL LEE TEEN CENTER.**

LaStacia Foster

I was so surprised to hear from Alex. I tried to find his e-mail address, but he never registered on classmates.com. My life after graduation has been pretty fulfilling. I decided shortly after leaving Ken Palmeiro that I wanted to help people in those kinds of crisis situations, so I became a social worker.

It is a high stress job, but it feels good to help people. I feel like I am someone there for kids to turn to in a crisis, and I like that feeling. I want kids to know there is someone out there willing to help them that they can trust.

I moved back to Junction City 6 months ago to become the full time counselor at the Jamal Lee Teen Center. I feel like all of us from 3-to-5 Program are still a Crew. We help each other out when one of us needs help. I was so happy to hear Alex's voice and I hope this is what he meant by an update of what we are doing.

I am still single and I hope to get into contact

with Patrick at our reunion. I have thought about him often since we graduated. I hope we might rekindle some of that flame that began to burn before we went our separate ways.

Nakeisha

I couldn't believe ol' oompa loompa be callin' me in the middle of the week. He be talkin' 'bout do I want to come and get together wit' The Crew? Boy don't know Nakeisha at all. I miss my Crew.

After graduation, I tried to be a rapper, but that shit didn't work. So I went to see Mr. T, my dawg. I told him how I tried to get into the rap industry and how they don't know me. Mr. T always cool and he told me the problem wasn't that they didn't know me. He said, "Nakeisha, it's not that they don't know you. It's not that people don't know you. The problem is that you don't know you."

Leave it to Mr. T to break it down like that. He reminded me that I had said I wanted to do hair for a living. He said he liked when I used to do the boys' hair before games and shit. I was like, yeah Mr. T, there ain't nobody 'roun here that do black people's hair professionally.

Now I do hair and nails. I make hella money too. My clients is mostly black, but I got some white chicks come in here wantin' they hair done. It's all about the Benjamins. I make mad cash.

Everyone know that I was the ring leader of our Crew and without me there wouldn't be no Crew. I made Senioritis our own word. Ain't nobody done it better than us, ever. We were the first; we were the last; we were the best. I remind people 'round here every day that I used to run the show.

Senioritis mean you wanna get out of that joint. It mean that you drivin' your teachers crazy. Senioritis is more than just not caring and shit. It is about making other people wish you was gone so they can move on with their lives without you.

Senioritis is a feeling that you leave behind. It is a feeling you have when you are at the crossroads in your life and you either make a good decision and do somethin' with yourself, or you become the bum they all think you is anyway. Senioritis is a feeling passed down from senior class to senior class that makes you want to leave so bad you wanna scream, but at the same time you don't wanna lose your friends and the situations you be in together.

We perfected senioritis and ain't nobody ever duplicated the mark we left on Junction City High School. Class of 2004 and the 3-to-5 Crew forever, fa sho!

The End